Was this temptation?

She glanced at Dan and, catching an unguarded, almost predatory look in his eyes, knew that it was. Still, she was powerless to pull her gaze from his, and a rush of heat made her long to seek his closeness, to touch and be touched—

Good heavens, what was she thinking? "I've got to go!"

Lisa was on her feet and bolting when Dan caught her wrist and stopped her.

"Do you know what I want?" he asked in a husky voice.

"N-no...." Lisa licked her lips. Then, light-headed from the wine, she raised herself on tiptoe and waited as Dan dipped his head and slowly lowered his mouth to hers. It felt so right—

Wrong! This is wrong! The words broke her dreamy haze. Lisa jerked out of Dan's embrace, hooked a foot around one of his calves and, with the speed and ease that come from years of practice, flipped Daniel Morgan smartly onto his backside.

Dear Reader:

All of us here at Silhouette Books hope that you are having a wonderful summer, and enjoying all that the season has to offer. Whether you are vacationing, or spending the long, warm summer evenings at home, we wish you the best—and hope to bring you many happy hours of romance.

August finds our DIAMOND JUBILEE in full swing. This month features *Virgin Territory* by Suzanne Carey, a delightful story about a heroine who laments being what she considers "the last virgin in Chicago." Her handsome hero feels he's a man with a mission—to protect her virtue *and* his beloved bachelorhood at the same time. Then, in September, we have an extraspecial surprise—*two* DIAMOND JUBILEE titles by two of your favorite authors: Annette Broadrick with *Married?!* and Dixie Browning with *The Homing Instinct*.

The DIAMOND JUBILEE—Silhouette Romance's tenth anniversary celebration—is our way of saying thanks to you, our readers. To symbolize the timelessness of love, as well as the modern gift of the tenth anniversary, we're presenting readers with a DIAMOND JUBILEE Silhouette Romance each month, penned by one of your favorite Silhouette Romance authors.

And that's not all! This month don't miss Diana Palmer's fortieth story for Silhouette—*Connal*. He's a LONG, TALL TEXAN out to lasso your heart! In addition, back by popular demand, are Books 4, 5 and 6 of DIANA PALMER DUETS—some of Diana Palmer's earlier published work which has been unavailable for years.

During our tenth anniversary, the spirit of celebration is with us year-round. And that's all due to you, our readers. With the support you've given us, you can look forward to many more years of heartwarming, poignant love stories.

I hope you'll enjoy this book and all of the stories to come. Come home to romance—Silhouette Romance—for always!

Sincerely,

Tara Hughes Gavin
Senior Editor

ANNE PETERS

Through Thick and Thin

Silhouette *Romance*

Published by Silhouette Books New York

America's Publisher of Contemporary Romance

To Monica Bracken
with gratitude for her time and patience.
And to my son, Robert Hansen,
with love and many thanks.

SILHOUETTE BOOKS
300 E. 42nd St., New York, N.Y. 10017

ISBN: 0-373-08739-X

First Silhouette Books printing August 1990

Printed in the U.S.A.

Books by Anne Peters

Silhouette Desire

Like Wildfire #497

Silhouette Romance

Through Thick and Thin #739

ANNE PETERS

has either lived or traveled in virtually every part of the world, but her roots are firmly planted in Pacific Northwest soil now. A mother—and grandmother—of two, she lives with her sales manager husband in Renton, Washington. When not writing, she reads, gardens, baby-sits her grandchildren or travels—and has even been known to do housework at times.

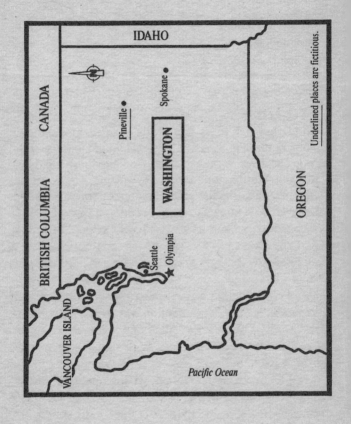

Underlined places are fictitious.

Chapter One

Hey, Nick. Drop what you're doing and give me a hand, will you?"

The request was issued with low-voiced urgency by a dark-haired slip of a girl in shabby jeans, and addressed to a young salesclerk rearranging a display of ivory-handled shoehorns.

Lisa Hanrahan didn't take time to look back and see if Nick was following. Her attention was riveted on the large man hurrying out of the store. Her concentration was focused entirely on catching him. With a final burst of speed she managed to overtake him out on the sidewalk.

"Just a minute, sir," she said, willing steel into the usually mellow timbre of her voice and ignoring the fierce drumming of her heart. Even after three years on the job, that flutter of fear at this moment of confrontation, that rush of adrenaline, never diminished. Only training and self-discipline enabled her to keep her gaze level and her stance assertive as she fumbled in her pocket for her ID card and badge.

The man, some ten inches taller and twice her weight, brushed her aside and walked on.

"Stop!" Incensed, Lisa spun around and overtook him again, badge aloft and Nick at her side at last. "Store security. Do you have a receipt for that wallet in your coat pocket?"

The man blanched. He gaped at the proffered badge. Lisa shot a quick glance at Nick, who looked uncomfortable. Well, he's no hero, she thought with a touch of exasperation, but then it was hoped neither one of them would have to be. For now, his mere presence was reassuring.

The man in front of her suddenly moved his arm and made to reach into the pocket of his shapeless tan raincoat. Lisa tensed, her full attention immediately back on the suspect. Unlikely as it seemed, she couldn't risk the chance that his hand might come out pointing a gun or a knife. She clamped down on his wrist and arrested the movement.

"Hold it," she ordered. "Keep your hands where I can see them."

"I was just gonna get the damn billfold," the man growled with a shrug. "I'll give it back and good riddance. Hell, I only forgot to pay for it."

"Yeah." Lisa had heard that particular line too often to give it much credence. "I guess you did."

Next he'll say he's never done anything like this before, she thought with uncharacteristic cynicism as she accepted the slim eel-skin wallet he handed her. How refreshing a simple admission of guilt would be for a change. But those were rarely forthcoming, and it had to be a sign of approaching burnout for her to wish it were otherwise.

"Let's go." Taking hold of his arm, she turned to escort the shoplifter back to the store. The man balked and tried to shake her off. Nick, not much bigger than Lisa herself, sidled closer and strove for a look of menace.

"Look, mister..." Lisa fixed her captive with a narrow-eyed gaze while her free hand fished for the handcuffs she carried in the back pocket of her jeans. "You can come with us quietly or I can slap these bracelets on you and drag you inside. It's up to you."

"What seems to be the trouble here?"

Hearing the unexpected male voice at her back, Lisa spared a quick glance over one shoulder and found herself confronted by the lightest pair of blue eyes she'd ever seen. Electric blue. The description popped into her mind as her hand unconsciously loosened its hold on the suspect, who seized the moment and made a run for it. Which was all it took to snap Lisa out of her momentary trance.

Whirling, she sprinted after him. The man's longer but older and heavier legs were no contest for Lisa's young and fleet ones. She tackled him from behind and stuck like a leech until he stopped moving. As soon as he did, she snapped the handcuffs around his wrists and, with a huffing Nick flanking his other side, began to alternately drag and push him back toward the store.

The man with the blue eyes, the one responsible for her momentary and unheard-of loss of concentration, again blocked their path. He, too, had joined in the short chase but was not even breathing hard.

"Look here," he said, "I'm—"

"No. You look here." Lisa cut him short more heatedly than she might have ordinarily, but her reaction to the man's eyes had unnerved her and she blamed him for the shoplifter's near escape. She shoved her badge beneath his nose.

"I'm Morgan Security and you, sir, are interfering with an arrest. There is no trouble unless you make it, so please just go about your business."

And with that she redoubled her hold on her captive's arm, sidestepped and shouldered him around the non-plussed would-be samaritan, and hurried toward the store entrance. She hoped the stranger would take the hint and go away, but there was no way she was going to look back to make sure.

"Thanks, Nick," she said to the salesman, who had hurried ahead to push open the big plate-glass door. "I really appreciate your help."

Hustling the suspect ahead of her, Lisa stepped into the store. Several shoppers had gathered to watch their arrival and progress, their faces alight with avid curiosity and speculation. Ignoring them, Lisa hurried the shoplifter along.

He appeared to have resigned himself to his lot and offered no further resistance. "Where're we going?" he asked.

"Upstairs."

Lisa briskly ushered him toward the single elevator in the back corner of Men's Fashions. As she did, she wished, not for the first time, that management would deign to listen to the staff's objections about the location of their security office. To have it on the fifth floor with the rest of the administrative and executive offices might make for a tidy arrangement housekeepingwise, but it was a damned inconvenient place for the agents to operate from.

Well. She punched "up." It wouldn't be her problem much longer, and she was glad.

The elevator arrived, the door wheezed open, and they entered.

Daniel Jefferson Morgan, Jr., as of that day the new manager of the Seattle branch of Morgan's Department Store, stood on the sidewalk where he'd just been so summarily dismissed.

A security agent, he thought incredulously. That pint-size ragamuffin was a Morgan security agent. Turner must have been desperate when he hired that one. Or else bewitched by those huge dark eyes.

As you were?

Slowly Dan walked back into the store, annoyance creasing his forehead. Those gypsy eyes were pretty spectacular, he grimly conceded, and they had certainly jolted his senses for an instant with their flash and fire. But not for a moment was he about to forget that they were set in the face of someone who could barely have reached the age of consent. If that.

"Problems?"

At his father's question, Dan looked up from his sightless contemplation of the store's maroon carpeting. D. J. Morgan, Sr., with various department heads in tow, had been touring the store with Dan before the latter had so abruptly left to chase after the girl. Now the group was gathered near the entrance, waiting to continue.

"What?" Dan's smile was slightly absentminded as he forced himself to focus on the man in front of him. "Oh. No. No problem, I guess. I thought there might be, but that . . . that *girl* seemed to have the situation under control when I got there." He frowned at his father. "Do you know her, by any chance?"

"Hanrahan, you mean?" Morgan, Sr., General Manager and Chief Executive Officer, chuckled. "Oh, yes, I know her. We all do, don't we, gentlemen?"

Murmurs of assent and somewhat indulgent smiles were evident all around. Dan's frown deepened.

"She's a bit of a maverick," his father continued, "not your run-of-the-mill agent, but Turner has nothing but praise for her."

"Really?" Dan could see that the entire entourage was smitten. They all looked like fond uncles with silly grins on their faces. "She hardly looks old enough to be out of high school," he pointed out, "much less work here. I'll have to have a chat with Turner first thing."

The others had lost their smiles and were conferring among themselves. "She's in her early twenties, I believe, sir," one of the younger department heads declared. "Been here a couple of years or so."

"Really?" Dan said again, frankly doubtful that the age given was correct. "Well, she's not quite my idea of a Morgan's security agent."

"Oh?" D.J. Sr.'s eyebrows rose. "In what way is she wrong?"

"In every way that matters." Dan did not think this was the time or the place to elaborate on the subject. "I've noticed that several departments are in dire need of change around here, Dad, but I'm beginning to think that security is the prime candidate." He shot his father a faintly challenging look. "I believe it is my prerogative as the new chief to institute whatever changes I deem necessary?"

"By all means," the older man assured him, "make all the changes you want. After all, if I didn't have faith in your judgment, I wouldn't be turning the reins of this, our biggest store, over to you. And security—not here so much as in some of our other branches—has been a concern to all of us on the board. Anchorage in particular is having major problems that are costing us very real losses. The situation needs dealing with, and anything you can come up with will be helpful. But remember this, Sonny—"

He placed an arm around his son's shoulders and lowered his voice. "Before you change too many things around, consult with your department heads. Get their input."

At this bit of gratuitous paternal caution, Dan stifled a rueful sigh and an exasperated shake of the head. He might be thirty-two years old, and he might have a marketing degree and several years of business management experience under his belt, but he supposed to his father he would always be Sonny and in need of advice.

"Shall we get on with the tour?" he invited mildly. "Ladies' Shoes was next, I believe, and doing very well. Simons tells me..."

With his father's arm still clasped around his shoulder, he and Dan, Sr. brought up the rear as the managerial procession moved sedately onward.

The first thing a visitor saw upon entering the security center was what looked like a wall of black-and-white television sets, all playing different programs. These televisions were, in fact, the latest in a string of devices employed by Morgan's, and other stores like them, in their ceaseless and costly war against shoplifting. Watched by security agents, these closed-circuit monitors transmitted, and could be made to record, the ongoing activities on the sales floor of every department via strategically placed video cameras.

The man in Lisa's custody seemed fascinated by this display of state-of-the-art detecting. He craned his neck and dragged his feet, but Lisa steered him relentlessly through a connecting door into a larger room housing several littered desks, two typewriters and a few chairs.

She hooked the back of one of them and pulled it next to a desk.

"Sit down," she ordered, extracting a set of keys from one of her pockets to unlock the handcuffs on the suspect's wrists. "And don't try anything cute."

She dropped the shoplifted eel-skin wallet onto the desk as she rounded it to take a seat on the other side. She cleared a space and pulled some forms out of a drawer. Then she picked up a printed card and looked the suspect in the eye.

"I'm going to read you your rights now." She cleared her throat. "You have the right to remain silent. You have the right at this time—"

"Aw, lady, come on," the man broke in with a whine. "What are you doin' this for?" He picked up the billfold and slapped it down again. "I'm tellin' you, I only forgot to pay for this thing. And you got it back, didn't ya?"

Lisa eyed him sternly. "Look, the law says I have to read you this, so please listen. You have the right at this time to an attorney of your own choosing," she repeated the phrase she had started to read, going on to reiterate his rights as guaranteed under the Miranda ruling and closing with the statement, "You have also been advised by me, Lisa Rose Hanrahan, that anything you say can, and will, be used against you in a court of law."

Lisa raised her eyes from the printed card and looked again at the distressed man. He looked more like a cornered rabbit than a desperate criminal, she thought. But she ruthlessly squelched the stirrings of sympathy that threatened to ruin her professional detachment. Sympathy was misplaced here, she knew. Shoplifters were amply warned of the consequences of their actions: notices were prominently displayed all over the store. Shoplifting was theft and prosecution did not depend on the value of the item stolen. Neither the store nor the security agent could make exceptions. Still, she thought with a sigh, there were times when she wished she could.

"What is your name, sir?"

"Murphy. Walter Murphy."

"All right, Mr. Murphy, do you understand these rights as I have explained them to you?" she asked, keeping her voice and facial expression neutral.

"Would you listen to me, lady? This ain't necessary. I'm no criminal. Hell, I—"

"Look," Lisa broke in. "I need you to tell me if you understand your rights. That's the law. So, do you?"

"Okay, okay," he snapped. Apparently his emotions had taken a sudden shift away from anguished distress. "I understand my damn rights."

"Good. Then do you want to call your lawyer, or sign this waiver here before we talk?"

Lisa pushed a pen and the waiver form toward him, sure he would sign. Most suspects did unless they were big-time operators with a record, or when valuable merchandise was involved. Since shoplifting anything under $250 classified the offense as a misdemeanor, few attorneys ever got involved. Still, the formalities had to be observed.

The man glared at her. "My lawyer? Hell, I don't have no lawyer. I ain't no thief."

"Unfortunately for you, this wallet here says you are," Lisa countered tiredly, tapping an unpolished but neatly trimmed fingernail on the evidence that lay on the desk between them. As the man grabbed the pen, scrawled his name along the bottom of the form and thrust both back at her, she picked the billfold up and slowly turned it over in her hands.

"Eel-skin," she mused aloud, shaking her head at the stupidity of it all. "Pretty, but not exactly one of life's necessities, is it, Mr. Murphy? And—" She tossed the thing back down. "If you ask me, at what—fifty, sixty bucks?— one helluva thing to get a police record for."

Murphy made no response, nor had Lisa expected one. She reached for the phone.

"Time to call in the cops," she explained as she dialed. "That, too, Mr. Murphy, is the law."

By the time Murphy and the police officer had gone their separate ways, Lisa had a blinding headache. She pinched the bridge of her nose, then let her hand drop. Eyes closed, she leaned back in the chair. Her shift was over, she would just relax a minute before she had to be on her way.

She lifted her feet onto the desk, slid down until she rested on her tailbone and sighed. If, at age twenty-four, it didn't sound so ridiculous, she'd say she was getting too old for this. Where was the exhilaration, the satisfaction of a job well-done? She used to feel that her work was important, especially during those times when apprehending and lecturing some youthful culprit steered him back onto the straight and narrow. But these days . . .

These days the seemingly endless procession of big and little crooks parading through her working life did nothing but depress her. It would feel so good to kiss this job good-bye in three months. To not have to count every nickel any-more or to shop at those thrift shops the smell of which would probably never leave her nostrils. And goodbye Mac'n Cheese, endless hot dogs and—yuck—*sardines*! Goodbye study, study, study. Hello, social life.

Lisa folded her hands across the hollow of her stomach and crossed her feet at the ankles. Of course, without all that studying, and without the academic scholarships that had precluded her playing hooky and failing the mark, she wouldn't now be eyeballing an ace position in the computer industry, would she?

She was being courted by, among others, the most dy-namic of computer software firms, Misotec. And after a lifetime of fending for herself, and—Lisa snorted—having to prove and assert herself *everywhere* because of her dis-gustingly infantile looks, that was quite an ego stroker. Oh, yeah . . .

The sound of a throat being energetically cleared roused her from her reverie. She dropped her hands off her stom-ach and, lifting her head just a little, opened one eye. She directed it balefully toward the balding man framed in the doorway. John Turner, her friend and, as security manager, her boss.

"Go away, John," she said without inflection, and allowed her eye to close again. "I'm out to lunch."

In view of the fact that they'd had lunch together hours ago, she expected his usual smart-mouthed comeback, but only silence greeted her pronouncement. A kind of heavy silence.

Puzzled, she sent another one-eyed look toward the door and—snapped upright. John wasn't alone. Towering in the doorway behind him and glaring at her with patent disapproval was the tall, blue-eyed busybody she had given those marching orders to out in front of the store. Good Lord.

Scrambling to her feet, Lisa straightened her shoulders and pulled herself up to her full five-feet-nothing height. Now what? she thought with her mind in a whirl. Had the guy registered a complaint against her because she'd been less than polite out there? Probably. He looked the type, sort of self-righteous, as if he were used to having people scrape and bow before him.

"Is anything wrong?" she asked, struggling with the tone of polite deference Morgan's store policy demanded of their employees when dealing with customers. Lisa had never been too good with that tone, which was why she had lasted only three months as a salesclerk.

Now she added a small smile and hoped for the best as the man stepped around John and pinned her with those disturbing eyes of his.

"Should there be something wrong?" he drawled, adding, "Miss, uh, Hanrahan," after checking the name on the file folder he carried in one hand.

Lisa stiffened and could actually feel the fine hairs at the back of her neck rising. That manila file obviously had her name on it. It was in *his* hand. Who was this stuffed shirt? She shot John Turner a glance that clearly reflected the unvoiced question if his immediate look of alarm was any indication. He rushed to her side.

"Lisa Hanrahan, may I present Daniel Morgan, Jr.," he announced with such rapid-fire formality that Lisa and Dan stared at him in amazement.

Brows arched, Lisa turned back to the man in the starched three-piece suit. He was tall, six feet, if he was an inch. And she had to concede that every one of those lean inches radiated the kind of confidence and power only money and breeding could instill. His face was dominated by those eyes—eyes that fascinated and drew her even as they seemed to look, oh, so coolly, down that chiseled hook of a nose of his. A nose just like the Old Man's . . .

"Daniel Morgan?" she more breathed than articulated before her mind clicked properly into gear. "Junior? *The*, uh, Junior?"

"To the best of my knowledge there's only one of us, yes."

The smile that suddenly lightened Daniel Morgan's stern features was a stunner. Lisa's large eyes grew larger still. Why, he's absolutely gorgeous, she thought. As Marcia would say, capital *G*, capital *O*, capital—

John's forceful clearing of the throat abruptly ended the spelling bee.

"Huh? Oh! N-nice to meet you." Good Lord, she'd finally gone over the edge from too much studying. Why else would she be acting like a blithering nitwit?

To add insult to injury, she felt herself blush. She, who never blushed, who had made a career out of cultivating a tough wise-guy facade to compensate for that terminally cute exterior of hers. It was humiliating. What must Morgan think of her?

As a matter of fact, Dan Morgan was thinking that Miss Hanrahan was looking quite adorable right at that moment. All rosy and flustered, rather like a pink bantam hen. Unfortunately, she also looked less like a Morgan's security person than ever. His smile was replaced by a thoughtful frown as he contemplated her.

He wanted Morgan's to be more than just another department store, and that meant they had an image to foster. An image of understated good taste in all things. An image of refinement and class not only for their merchandise but for their staff, as well.

His father had gotten lax in maintaining that image. He, Dan, intended to rectify that at this store, at least. Under *his* management strict standards of conduct, attitude and overall appearance would be established and enforced.

Dan eyed Lisa critically. She stood beside the littered desk and stared back at him with her straight little nose rising up in the air. Look at her, he thought, eighty pounds soaking wet, if that. He mentally shook his head at the defiance that radiated from her like heat from a potbellied stove. Eyes burning like coals in a pixie face devoid of makeup; a thick mop of dark hair, tousled but reassuringly shiny.

Miss Hanrahan was clean, he'd give her that, but hardly neat. The jeans she wore had holes at the knees, had faded to drabness and encased her too-slender form like a second skin. A pink shirttail hung out from under a once-red sweatshirt the sleeves of which had been hacked off at the elbows.

Dan shifted his critical gaze to her feet and inwardly shuddered. Those sneakers. Their original color was a mystery... and it would be impossible to adequately describe their present shade. But there was no mistaking the redness of the sock sticking out through the large hole in front.

No, he decided grimly, Turner's high opinion of her notwithstanding, Lisa Hanrahan would not do as a Morgan's security agent. If possible another, less visible position would have to be found for her.

He lifted his gaze. It collided with hers and stuck.

Lisa had conducted her own thorough inspection of Dan Morgan while he had been studying her like some distasteful, alien species. She noted the high forehead, and thought that those prominent cheekbones, that proud nose and firmly etched mouth made him look like one of the Greek warriors she had seen depicted in history texts. Spartans, that was it. Fierce.

Certainly one good-looking man, she grudgingly admitted, though his looks did nothing to endear him to her. On the contrary, locking eyes with him and reading in his only disapproval and a sort of pitying regret, she almost hated him. He was going to make things unpleasant for her, she just knew it.

All right, so be it. He was the boss. Lisa rallied her defenses like a general his troops. Two could play the unpleasantness game.

Outwardly calm, inwardly already seething, she watched his eyes briefly widen as if in recognition of her thoughts. One dark blond eyebrow rose at a slant, giving him a kind of rakish look that hinted of a challenge accepted.

Good.

Breaking eye contact, he pulled up a chair and sat down. "Now then, Miss Hanrahan," he said briskly, crossing his legs and absently adjusting the knife-edged crease of his trousers. "I'd like to talk to you a moment about your position—"

"Do you mind if I sit too, Mr. Morgan?" Asking, Lisa smiled the kind of smile that had John Turner shifting uneasily from foot to foot.

"What?" Morgan seemed a bit disconcerted by the request, as though he belatedly realized he should have offered her a seat right away. "No, of course not," he added. "Please, do."

He cleared his throat, smoothed his tie. "As I was about to say, Miss Hanrahan, regarding your—"

"Thank you. And excuse me." Lisa noisily dragged the chair from behind the desk before perching primly on its edge. "It's been a long day."

Morgan's brows descended to shade narrowing eyes as he watched her squirm and fidget on the chair, trying to get comfortable.

"Miss Hanrahan, if you don't mind, I'd like to get on with this." He flipped open her file with barely leashed impatience. "Now. About your position in—"

"Mind?" Lisa rounded her eyes as wide as she could. "Of *course* I don't mind. I'm in quite a hurry myself. In fact—" she made a production of consulting her watch "—my shift ended thirty minutes ago, so I'm going to have to clock overtime—"

"Fine."

The word was fired like a pistol shot, and Lisa noted with satisfaction that Dan Morgan's ultracorrect facade was crumbling. His face was turning pink, and the look he sent her was fulminating.

John seemed to be trying to get her attention, but Lisa ignored him and concentrated on looking cool and demure in spite of the fiery volcano roiling inside her. Damn, but she detested new bosses who thought they had to throw their weight around the first day on the job. It gave her great pleasure to watch Dan Morgan's aristocratic nostrils flare as he took a deep breath and tried again.

"If you could spare a few moments of your attention, Miss Hanrahan," he said with obviously hard-won patience, "this shouldn't cut too deeply into your undoubtedly valuable free time. As it is, I haven't had a chance to really study your personnel file, nor to fully discuss the matter with Turner here, but just for the record I—"

"Excuse me, Mr. Morgan, I really hate to interrupt again but I do have an appointment." Lisa struggled for a look of apologetic innocence. "Is this going to take long?"

"Not at all." His patience clearly history, Morgan slammed her file shut and surged to his feet. "Quite the contrary, Miss Hanrahan, we're through."

His back rigid with fury, he stalked to the door and wrenched it open. He turned to glare back at Lisa, who sat unmoving. With eyes drilling into hers like ice-blue laser beams, he pronounced, "You're fired."

Chapter Two

John Turner was the first to break the stunned silence that followed Dan Morgan's stormy departure.

"Smooth, Lisa," he drawled sarcastically, "real smooth."

"Well, darn it," she spluttered, "that man is absolutely... I mean, what was I supposed to do when—"

Catching John's forbidding expression and slow, negative shake of his head, Lisa aborted the rest of her defensive tirade. Her shoulders slumped. "Shoot," she said feelingly, "I blew it, didn't I?"

John's nod was heartfelt. "Yup."

"Dumb, huh?"

"Yup."

"What do you think I ought to do?"

"Do?" John rocked back on his heels and seemed to consider the question. "Offhand I'd say you've already done quite enough, wouldn't you?"

He abruptly shifted his weight to the balls of his feet and pierced her with a ferocious stare. "Dammit to hell, Leece, did you have to go out of your way to antagonize the man? Couldn't you have kept your pride locked up, your mouth zipped and just listened? It's bad enough you look like a rag doll that's losing its stuffing, couldn't you at least have conducted yourself like a professional, for crying out loud?''

His tone immediately put Lisa on the defensive again. ''Sure,'' she cried, leaping up off her chair. ''I should have just sat there like a good little girl while he raked me over the coals for no reason at all, is that it? And don't *you* start on my clothes, John Turner, when it's all your fault.''

Outrage making her movements jerky, Lisa yanked down her shirttail and started shoving it into her pants, muttering, ''Come in right away, Leece, you said. Come as you are, Leece, you said, I need you pronto. . . .''

Her hands gave up their fight with the shirttail, and her eyes shot black flames at Turner. ''It's my day off and I was papering the john when you called all in a panic. And you said you'd stick me on the monitors, that no one would see me. Ha!'' She tossed her head. ''Look what your word got me. . . .''

''My word, Leece?'' John fumed. ''*My* word? Seems to me, sweetheart, it was *your* words got you canned. And I don't think your clothes had a thing to do with it.''

''Humph! Maybe you didn't see the way he looked at me! Those were not compliments I read in his eyes, my friend.''

''So now she reads eyes,'' John declared disgustedly. ''Swell. Try reading my lips, kid. You blew it.''

''I already said so, didn't I?'' Lisa was tired of fighting. At the best of times it wasn't something she enjoyed for longer than it took to vent some steam. And John was right—all she was doing was trying to justify the unjustifiable.

She blew out a noisy breath and glumly contemplated the floor. "God, what a mess. I really don't need this now, you know...?"

She fell silent, noted the big toe and red sock sticking out of her sneaker and tried to curl them back inside. Unable to do so, she looked up at John again. "Something about that man irks me. He's so...I don't know, so condescending, so typically *rich*..."

"So what if he is?" John exclaimed. "Who cares? He's the boss, dammit."

"I know he's the boss, John. He just demonstrated that little fact very effectively by firing me."

"Can you really blame him?"

"I guess not." Lisa grimaced. "I acted like an a—"

"—dolescent brat," John finished for her. "Yeah, you did. Question is, what're you planning to do about it?"

"Apologize?" she hazarded. The word nearly choked her. Humility had never been her strong suit, much to her father's sorrow. *Humility goes before honor,* he would quote in one of his Sunday sermons, and his eyes would rest on his too-proud youngest child. *Humble yourself before the Lord and He will exalt you,* he would preach, but Lisa never quite succeeded. Which had been one of the reasons she had left the country parsonage that had been her childhood home just as soon as she graduated from high school.

Apologize. It pained her to even think the word but, try as she might, she could think of no other way out of this fiasco. Swallowing her pride like a bitter pill, she asked, "Can you get me an appointment, or should I do it myself?"

"I'll do it," John grumbled. "And I wouldn't do this for anybody else. But maybe if I explain to him about your master's and about those job offers—"

"Oh, no!" Lisa interrupted with instant heat. "No way! I will not be kept on here by an act of charity."

"Charity? Don't be ridiculous, charity. It's not—"

"No! John, I mean it." Lisa clutched his arm and shook it. "Promise you won't tell Morgan anything about those offers. Promise."

"Okay, okay, you're breaking my arm."

"Just ask if he'll see me, that's all."

John rubbed the back of his neck and slanted her a piercing look of warning. "No surprises, you hear me? No funny stuff, no getting on soapboxes about how wealth is wasted on the rich and all that."

"Right."

"Okay, then. I'll talk to him." He dropped his arm, sighed and slowly headed for the door. "You going to class tonight?"

"No. Just KP at the downtown mission."

"You still doing that?"

"Yup. Twice a week." Lisa darted over to another desk and, grabbing a bulging green backpack, followed John out of the room. "And I'm late already—I wasn't kidding when I told Morgan I had to be somewhere. Dinner starts in less than an hour and I was supposed to help get it ready."

"You? Cook?" John snorted. "Those winos and bums are lucky you're late."

"Ha-ha, very funny. Anyway, I didn't say anything about doing the cooking, just helping." She playfully punched his arm as she trotted past and out the door of the monitor room, only to immediately stick her head back in. "I should be home around nine or, if not, just leave a message with Marcia, will you?"

"Since when is she home at that hour? She reforming?" John called after her.

Lisa laughed without looking back, waving an arm. "No. Just broke, like me."

Dan Morgan stepped back into his office, unseen by the young woman jogging toward the escalator. Her shirttail was still hanging out, he thought with a frown. But it was the vision of Lisa Hanrahan's dancing eyes, gleaming teeth and laughing lips that lingered to disturb him.

The next morning, at exactly two minutes to ten, Lisa walked into the outer office of the executive suite. John had roused her from sleep at the crack of dawn to say he had been successful in smoothing Dan Morgan's ruffled feathers and that she was to present herself promptly at ten.

At her arrival, Doris, the middle-aged secretary Dan had inherited along with his lofty position, looked up from her typing with a professional smile that swiftly changed to one of amazement.

"Lisa?" she hazarded.

Lisa peered out from beneath the brim of her black felt hat and grinned. "I know, it's a shock. Marcia did my makeup."

Doris's comprehending nod was as hesitant as her smile. "That's quite an outfit, too," she murmured.

Lisa's grin widened as she did a quick pirouette. "You like it?"

She had dressed with care for the upcoming interview, wanting to rectify the unfavorable impression she knew she had created the day before. The black oversize and unstructured linen blazer, white collarless shirt and multihued silk scarf had all been lucky finds in the secondhand shops she frequented. She wore them with a long, loosely fitted black linen skirt and ballet slippers, and had been told the ensemble gave her a certain gamin elegance.

Now, with one hand in the skirt's pocket, she struck an exaggerated modeling pose. "Well, dahling?" she vamped.

"Well." Doris blinked and shook her head, but seemed unable to come up with any further commentary. Neither of them noticed Dan Morgan's approach.

"Miss Hanrahan, I presume?" he said in bone-dry tones, planting himself in front of Lisa, one eyebrow arched.

Giving him a weak smile, Lisa hurried to align legs and pelvis less provocatively. She felt waves of heat wash over her face and prayed the layers of makeup would hide the irritating blush. They didn't.

Morgan's eyes traveled her features with the intensity of electric-blue sensors. His lips twitched as he added, "Let me guess—right after our meeting you're on your way to audition for a part in *My Fair Lady*, is that it? Eliza Doolittle, perhaps?"

Lisa's chagrin at having been caught posing for Doris gave way to affront. Eliza Doolittle, indeed. Did he think she was some ignorant nobody in need of tutoring and a handout from the likes of him?

She inhaled sharply and stuck out her chin, about to let loose with a scathing rejoinder but, finding her gaze trapped in the twinkling brightness of his, was unable to do anything but softly exhale again.

He was teasing her, she realized. And she, who thought there was little that could stump her, was stumped.

"Please come in," Dan said, and wordlessly Lisa entered.

Once inside, Dan took his time rounding the massive oak desk and lowering himself into the age-softened leather cushions of the swivel chair behind it. He was stalling for time, delaying the moment when he would have to face the astounding, *confounding* young woman who had not given him a moment's peace of mind since he first laid eyes on her some twenty-four hours earlier.

He was stalling—fussily straightening already neatly aligned stacks of papers on his desk and aimlessly picking up and riffling through nameless files—because he wasn't at all sure he would be able to meet her eyes with the expression of somber authority he suspected the moment called for.

Lisa Hanrahan was here to apologize, after all, and although his ire had cooled hours ago and he'd even been able to chuckle about the incident somewhere in the wakeful hours of the night, he was not about to make things easy for her. And there was still the unexpectedly tabled matter of her unsuitability for his security team to be discussed.

Turner had intimated Miss Hanrahan might balk at a transfer to a less visible and risky position elsewhere in the store, but Dan felt sure he would have no trouble making her see the wisdom of it. As he saw it, Lisa might be unorthodox and somewhat zany in matters of dress and comportment...

Dan stifled the unwelcome chuckle that threatened to destroy his hard-won composure as he called to mind the outfit she was wearing right at that moment. Unorthodox, definitely, but he reminded himself that there could be no questioning her intelligence. It shone from her eyes like a beacon, besides being amply documented in the personnel file he was now making a project of scanning once again.

Other than the requisite vital statistics, it gave little insight into Lisa Rose Hanrahan, the person, except to state that she was a graduate student at the University of Washington. What it did contain were numerous commendations she had earned on the job for ideas to improve the effectiveness and efficiency of just about every aspect of the security department. There was no doubting her organizational talents and quick mind.

Since Morgan hadn't told her to sit, Lisa remained standing on the far side of the largest desk she had ever seen, and waited. She thought it rude, the way he needlessly fussed with stacks of papers and ignored her, but she supposed he meant to put her in her place just in case she'd mistaken his earlier joviality for forgiveness of her own rudeness the day before. An eye for an eye and all that. She guessed he was entitled, though it didn't make her mission of apology any easier. And she didn't much like him for that.

This was the first time Lisa had been inside one of the executive offices, but other than to briefly take note of the room's immense size and tasteful furnishings, she didn't bother to look around. Her attention was centered on the man behind the desk as her temper began to simmer, causing her good intentions to gradually evaporate.

Slipping her tiny shoulder bag off her arm, she gripped it in both hands. All right, she thought with gritted teeth, if that's how he wanted to play, she would just stand here and stare at him until he deigned to acknowledge her.

Honesty compelled her to admit that staring at the man was no hardship. He looked every inch the executive in a navy blue suit, crisp blue-and-white striped shirt and yellow tie. His brows were lowered at half-mast again, she noted. He certainly frowned a lot, at least around her. Annoyance? she speculated, adding irreverently, indigestion?

Something—a muscle tick?—briefly disturbed the rigid precision of his chiseled jaw, and the nostrils of his equally precise nose flared. Other than that, his face might have been carved from granite: angles and planes, with no hint of softness even in the lips that lay together in a straight line.

"Please have a seat, Miss Hanrahan."

Lisa hastily abandoned her contemplation and looked into the blueness of his eyes. For a moment their gazes locked and Lisa felt an odd tingling. Nerves, she decided with a hint of panic. Of all the times to get an attack of nerves.

"I—I'll stand, thank you."

Dan, too, was blinking in surprise at the surge of emotion he had experienced while looking into Lisa's eyes. He knew better than to call it nerves, though. What he would have called it, with any other woman, was physical attraction, sexual awareness, but the idea was ludicrous with regard to Lisa Hanrahan. True, she was not the teenager he had mistaken her for, but neither was she even remotely the kind of woman who could stir a man's blood. What she did stir up, besides acute irritation, were a man's sympathies—she was so damn vulnerable looking.

He tried for a smile and a reassuring word, but Lisa's rush of verbiage forestalled speech on his part.

"Mr. Morgan, I want to apologize for my behavior last night. It was out of line and I ask that you rescind the dismissal based on my heretofore unblemished record."

She drew an obviously relieved breath at the end of her apology and sat down.

Dan kept his smile merely cordial though amusement wanted to creep in. "Thank you, Miss Hanrahan," he said. "Apology accepted."

Lisa smiled, too. They studied each other in silence a moment. Dan took in her clothes once again and couldn't help but chuckle.

"That is quite an ensemble you have on."

Lisa sat up straighter and touched a small hand to the brim of her ridiculous hat. "Thank you," she said primly.

Her gratified response was totally disconcerting in that it made clear to Dan that she obviously took his words as a compliment rather than the gentle gibe he had intended. Nonplussed, he searched for a tactful way to clarify his meaning, knew there wasn't one and decided to shelve the matter altogether.

He picked up her file and once more riffled through it. "I see that you're a math and computer science major," he said on a different tack. "Hmm. Your master's must be nearly completed."

"It is."

"Expensive, isn't it?"

"A little." Lisa's short laugh emphasized the understatement of her reply. "I've had help, though."

"Your parents?"

"No." This time Lisa's laugh was unabashedly amused, but though Dan wished she would elaborate, she didn't. And he found himself reluctant to press.

"Scholarships?"

"That, and friends. And," she added, "Morgan's quite generous wages, of course."

Dan acknowledged the last with a small smile of his own. She was backhandedly reminding him that she needed the job he hadn't actually said was still hers. He decided he was human enough to enjoy letting her squirm just a little in retribution for causing his uncharacteristic loss of temper the day before.

"Any good jobs out there?"

"Well, yes, but..." Lisa hedged, and Dan wondered why the question seemed to discomfit her so. "I...I'm very happy where I am, for the time being," she finished in a rush.

"In security?"

"Definitely."

"And if I were to tell you I wanted you out of there, what would you say?"

"Why, I'd—" Lisa stared at him dumbfounded. They had been chatting so amiably, she had forgotten about their inherently adversarial relationship. Why, he'd been stringing her along, she thought indignantly. He had been playing her like a fish on a line only to slit her throat just as soon as she stopped fighting him. "I thought you had accepted my apology," she said stiffly now, her chin coming up.

"I have," Dan replied, telling himself to say what he meant to say and get it over with. Because it was fast becoming obvious to him that she might offer more resistance to his proposal than he had previously thought. "The one thing has nothing to do with the other. However, to continue our, uh, aborted discussion of last night, Miss Hanahan, let me begin by saying that as well as talking to Turner, I also discussed your record with my father. To your credit, they both think very highly of you. I have also studied your file at great length and am well aware of your accomplishments here and at the university. You are to be congratulated."

Even to himself he sounded like a pompous schoolmaster, and despite Lisa's carefully blank facial expression, Dan thought he could read a similar assessment in her eyes. To his chagrin, he was unable to come up with a lighter tone and grimly plowed on.

"The fact is, however, that your physical, uh, attributes are such that...I mean to say that physically you are bound to be at a disadvantage to almost anyone you attempt to arrest. And therefore—"

Damn. Did she have to look at him as if she thought he liked beating kids and animals, too? Dan stuck a finger inside his collar and pulled as if to loosen a noose he felt tightening around his throat.

"Look, Lisa," he said after a lengthy clearing of his throat, "you're an intelligent young woman. You'll see that what I am about to propose is nothing personal. There's a position open in accounting and I want you to take it. It's right up your alley," he hurried on, "qualificationswise. It pays somewhat better than security work and...well, you'll be less—"

"Visible, is that it?" Lisa's voice was rough with injured pride.

"Actually, I was going to say vulnerable, but since you mention visibility—yes, that is a factor, as well."

"I knew it!" Lisa's handbag fell to the floor as she sprang, infuriated, to her feet. "Well, let me tell you something, Mr. Morgan. Yesterday was my day off and I—"

"Turner already explained that," Dan cut her off sharply. He was glaring again and looking very unpleasant. "Sit down, Miss Hanrahan."

"No, thank you." Lisa planted both sets of knuckles on the edge of his desk and returned his glare across its vast expanse. "I am going to say this—"

"Sit down, Miss Hanrahan!" Dan Morgan, too, was on his feet now and clearly as angry as she.

Lisa stood her ground a moment longer, her dark eyes battling the ice-blue blast of his, then gave a small shrug and slowly sat back down.

Morgan remained as he was, and his eyes stayed fused to hers. Faced with all that outraged masculinity, Lisa felt a small tremor start in the pit of her stomach. It was a watered-down version of what she had felt the time she had climbed—on a dare from one of her brothers—all the way to the top of a towering maple. And looked down.

Her father had had to come up after her, pry her arms and legs off the limbs she was clinging to and carry her down like a baby. Once safely back on the ground, she had received a blistering lecture and been grounded socially, as well.

She had secretly climbed that tree again and again, battling the fear and the vertigo, vowing to overcome it, too stubborn to give up. And so now she could not back off, but met Morgan glower for glower.

"Miss Hanrahan," Dan finally said with visible restraint. "I don't mean to be unkind and I can appreciate your financial difficulties, but your mode of dress is not in keeping with the image I intend to establish for Morgan's. You have two choices: take that job in accounting or leave."

He sat down heavily.

"Wrong." Lisa popped up on her feet again. "I have a third choice, Mr. Morgan, and that is to stay where I am. And unless you hand out uniforms, I'll continue to dress as I have—cleanly, to be sure—but casually, just like everyone else in the department."

"Let me remind you that I have yet another option, too, Miss Hanrahan," Dan ground out, "one that at the moment I am strongly tempted to exercise. And that is to fire you. Again."

"In which case I'd be forced to fight you, Mr. Morgan, because you have no just cause for dismissal. From the minute you first saw me, you've judged my performance by impressions that have no bearing on my ability to do the job."

Lisa sat back down and folded her hands primly in her lap. She smiled at him, feeling pretty good. "I believe I'd win, too."

Dan's eyes blazed as he slowly rose from his chair again and leaned across the desk toward her. "Shall we put it to the test, Miss Hanrahan?"

"If you wish."

Morgan stared at her for long moments during which the dropping of a pin would have had the impact of a thunderclap. Lisa could hear the beat of her racing heart and wondered if Morgan could hear it, too. She felt an overwhelming need to blink her eyes, to swallow, to fidget in her seat, but dared do none of those things lest he interpret them as a loss of nerve.

And as she stalwartly returned his stare, she witnessed a slow and gradual melting of the ice, a softening of the rigid set of his jaw, a smoothing of his features into something less fierce yet no less implacable. He slowly straightened away from her and sat down.

Lisa felt the tension drain out of her. She waited for him to speak.

"Yesterday I made the mistake of acting in the heat of anger," he finally said, almost pleasantly. "I have no intention of doing so again." He consulted a small slip of paper. "According to Turner, you're not scheduled to work today or tomorrow. One of us will be in touch with you before you're due back at work. Good day."

With that he gave a short nod of dismissal, pushed aside Lisa's file and picked up another. Ignoring her, he immersed himself in it.

Lisa sat momentarily slack jawed and unmoving, not sure how she had been maneuvered into this state of limbo, but very certain that she didn't like it in the least. To gain time to catch her wits, she bent to pick her handbag up off the floor, then slowly got to her feet. She stood by the desk, still irresolute, when he looked up with raised brows.

"Was there anything else, Miss Hanrahan?"

A multitude of arguments, none of them coherent, leaped to her tongue. Yet, much as it galled her to do so, Lisa shook her head. "No."

"Well, then?"

She felt like hitting him, like taking him by the ears and shaking the stuffing right out of him, and it seemed he knew it. The beginnings of a smile brought sunshine to his face and thawed his glacial gaze as he slowly lounged back in his chair.

"Good day, Miss Hanrahan," he said softly.

Lisa stood her ground for another moment, warmed by his regard in spite of herself and strangely loathe to have it end. Then she angrily called herself to task. She spun away, the sharp motion making her hat slip its mooring. She yanked it off her head and stormed from the room, all the while unsuccessfully trying to close her ears to the sound of Dan Morgan's curiously gentle laughter.

Chapter Three

Lisa could hardly wait until Marcia came home that night so that she could unload on her all the clever retorts, incisive comments and cutting counterarguments she had kept dreaming up all day in response to Dan Morgan's cool dismissal. Marcia's twin brother, Marc, a fixture around the apartment more often than not, was paying his usual dinnertime visit and, between bites of chicken, was satisfactorily vocal in his support.

Up until that final moment in Morgan's office she had been doing so well, Lisa was saying. She had been holding her own, and then somehow, with little more than a flicker of the man's ridiculously long lashes, he'd had her down for the count.

"Well, not really down," she amended, tossing aside the chicken wing with which she had been stabbing the air. "Just knocked off balance." She wiped her hands on a paper napkin, then balled it up in her fist. "I tell you this, though, if Dan Morgan wants a fight, he's going to get one.''

"Yea, Lisa.''

"Way to go, babe.''

Lisa beamed at her fan club, gratified by their unquestioning acceptance of her version of the interview which, honesty compelled her to admit to herself, she had shaded somewhat for better effect.

"So what does John have to say about all this?'' Marcia asked, daintily gnawing on a drumstick, chartreuse-tipped pinky extended at right angles to the rest of her hand. A hairstylist, like her brother, she was always brilliantly colorful from the top of her—currently—silver-blond hair to her feet shod in unlaced purple high tops.

Lisa shrugged and sipped from her glass of milk. "I haven't talked to John since he phoned here in the wee hours, but at that time he still wasn't too thrilled with me. His position is: why rock the boat when you're planning to shortly abandon ship anyway?''

"What ship?'' Marcia said.

Accustomed to Marcia's literal bent, the other two ignored her interjection. Marc picked up another piece of chicken, his fourth.

"This isn't half-bad,'' he allowed, chewing with enjoyment. "And John has a point. Not that I'm not behind you a hundred percent, Leece,'' he hastened to add.

"I know that—on both counts.'' Sliding down from the antiquated kitchen stool she'd been sitting on, Lisa gathered up plates and cutlery, including Marc's, which promptly caused noisy protest. "Sorry,'' she said, crossing her arms and leaning back against the counter. "I forgot about that hollow leg of yours.''

She returned his grimace, then watched fondly as he polished off the last piece of chicken in the bucket. Marc and Marcia Bennett were more than friends to her—they had been like part of her family for almost seven years now. She loved them as she loved her parents and her brothers whom she saw all too rarely.

The three of them had shared it all, the good times and the bad. And had grown so much, come so far since they had first met at the same mission where Lisa still volunteered twice a week. Except the three of them had not been there as workers in those days, they had all been on the receiving end of the handouts.

Well . . . Lisa turned to run water into the sink for the few dishes they had dirtied with their simple take-out meal. They would not need handouts again if she could help it.

And she could. It simply meant swallowing her dumb pride for once and keeping her job—any job—at Morgan's until she was done with school and went to work for Misotec.

She slowly rubbed the dishrag over the plate, not seeing it, seeing Dan Morgan's face instead. Gently she moved the cloth over it again and again. She remembered the gradual relaxation of his rigid features during their final standoff, the soft laughter that had followed her out of his door and which, oddly, had not stung so much as warmed her.

And she suddenly sensed with certainty that, no matter what, Dan Morgan had no intention of firing her again.

The realization abruptly took the wind out of the sails of the battleship she had been prepared to launch. There was no need to fight him.

Her brow creased, and she raised her head to stare sightlessly out of the night-darkened window above the sink. And she knew what it was that she must—or, more precisely, must not—do. It had to do with the rocking of boats.

For most of the next day, Lisa was in class, either lecturing in her capacity of teaching assistant to one of the professors, or being lectured to herself. Between that and another stint at The Mission, there had been no chance to call Dan Morgan with her decision. Nor, by the time she staggered wearily into the apartment after ten o'clock that night, had he apparently found a moment to call her with his.

So, dressed in clean if threadbare jeans and a purple UW sweatshirt, she reported to security next morning as had been scheduled prior to her talk with Dan. She was immediately caught up in the madness that reigned there. Personal concerns were shelved.

There was a sale in Sportswear; representatives of several major cosmetics companies were doing complimentary make-overs on the first floor, and it was a school holiday. Consequently kids of all ages roamed everywhere, looking, touching, but only rarely buying. School holidays and vacations were always an especially hectic time for store security, as well as a time where shoplifting incidents skyrocketed.

Lisa and Bob Janssen, another agent, were practically cheek to cheek, bent over the close-up monitor, intent on the actions of a young boy in the Stereo Department.

The boy had been standing by the cassette tape display for some time, alternately picking up and laying down some of the merchandise. Every so often he would cast furtive glances over his shoulder, and once or twice they had watched him wipe apparently sweaty palms on the side of his jeans.

Lisa and Bob were sure he was up to no good. The signs were classic: this kid was going to steal. Yet when he did, they almost missed it. In the blink of an eye he had pocketed a cassette tape and was sauntering away from the display. One more glance over his shoulder and he started to sprint for the escalator.

Lisa was running even before the boy did, while Bob contacted John, who was cruising the sales floor somewhere, on the walkie-talkie. At the same time, he hurried to adjust knobs and buttons on the monitor in order to keep the kid on camera.

Lucky for them the Stereo Department was up on the fifth floor with the security office, Lisa thought as she too sped toward the escalator. Still, the kid had a head start and it was anybody's guess just where he would go. Unless Bob could keep him on camera and advise her of his whereabouts, she could only trust dumb luck to lead her to him. Lisa didn't much believe in luck.

She arrived on the fourth floor and looked around. Nothing. Instinct told her he had probably continued on down. He had been very nervous, which might mean that he hadn't done this kind of thing much, if at all. He would probably head for one of the exits, or get cold feet and dump the cassette somewhere.

"Lisa, do you read?"

Lisa ducked behind a dummy in diving gear and raised her walkie-talkie. "Go ahead."

"He's on third, heading down. Looks like he'll run for it. John's watching for him on first."

"Got it." She was off again, weaving through and around clusters of shoppers, taking downward steps two at a time. On the second floor, she saw the boy, right in front of her. Lisa pocketed her radio and slowed down. Together, one after the other, they descended to the first floor where she saw John unobtrusively watching them.

The boy was no longer running, but was obviously scared half out of his wits and heading for the nearest exit. Lisa was pretty sure he had not ditched the cassette tape, because Bob Janssen would likely have seen and reported it. She was also sure that the boy had no intention of paying for the thing, but she could not legally stop and challenge him until he and the merchandise had left the store.

She shot a glance over her shoulder at John who gave an almost imperceptible nod. Catching the door as the boy released it, she went out after him.

"Hold it, kid," Lisa called, badge already extended. "Store security. You have a cassette tape in your pocket you didn't pay for...."

John was holding the door for them as she led the sullen boy back into the store.

Daniel Morgan walked into the security office while Lisa and John were still dealing with the boy. Standing quietly in a corner, he listened to Lisa's lecture. John Turner had done little else than sing her praises the past two days. Here was his chance to judge her work for himself.

In the course of some soul-searching the past forty-eight hours, Dan had been forced to admit to himself that his decision to remove Lisa from security had been based on emotions. Emotions that ranged from latent chauvinism and a need to establish his authority to genuine concern and a baffling compulsion to shield the woman from life's less pleasant aspects. None of them, he realized, were valid reasons for tampering with an employee's job. Nor were they worthy considerations for the kind of employer he hoped and strove to be.

Focusing on Lisa now, he felt the urge to smile. Being around her did that to him, though he wasn't sure why. Perhaps her feistiness amused him just as her courage to speak out and to stand up for herself impressed him—when it wasn't making him furious.

Turner, as well as Dan's father, thought Lisa Hanrahan the logical choice for the thing he was planning for Anchorage. Dan eyed her critically, inwardly wincing at the jeans and sweatshirt she wore. He decided he wasn't ready to commit himself to her quite that much yet. He would bide his time, keep an eye on her, see how things shaped up. Meanwhile . . .

"We had to call your mother away from work," he heard her say sternly to her young captive, "away from sick people who need her to be there. You're a big boy—nine, did you say? Your mom trusted you to behave, pal. And what about your dad? He's a fisherman, right? How do you think he'd feel if he knew you were stealing while he's out there making a living for you?"

Lisa stopped talking and looked at the boy—Pete, he had said his name was—then seemed about to say something else. Apparently changing her mind, she turned to John Turner and threw her hands up in the air.

"I'm sorry," she announced dramatically, "I can't talk to this kid. He's too much like my cousin."

Her cousin? Dan's attention sharpened.

Pete too stopped sniveling into his collar and squinted up at her with worried curiosity creasing his freckled forehead.

John took over. "Mike, you mean?" He shook his head sorrowfully and looked at Pete, who was growing visibly more alarmed. "Yeah, I see what you mean. First, it was just little things with him, too, wasn't it? Cassettes, right? Just like this one." He held the evidence aloft. "But it didn't stop there, did it. No, sir!"

John paused as if overcome. "Before you knew it, it was grand theft auto and he's doing ten to fifteen at Sing Sing."

Lisa nodded, a faraway look of sadness in her eyes. "Sing Sing," she repeated softly. "Guys have been known to get killed in places like that."

She seemed to rally herself. Dan was riveted by the entire performance. Pete had grown pale. "K-killed?" he quaked.

Lisa clasped him around the shoulders, a tiny smile on her face as she brought it close to his. "Yeah," she said, "killed.

But—'' She straightened and clapped him heartily on the back. "That won't happen to you, will it, Pete?"

Pete's shake of the head was tentative. "It won't?" he squeaked.

"Naw." John jumped back into the dialogue like an actor on cue. "Course it won't. Because you're no dummy like Mike was, are you, Pete? You're not ever gonna steal again, are you? Why, even if you didn't go to Sing Sing, they'd for sure put you in some lousy jail with rats and bugs—and stuff like tuna casserole for dinner."

"I kinda like tuna casserole," Pete said.

Amid the burst of laughter that followed, Dan slipped out again, undetected.

When the doorbell rang, Lisa was sprawled on the living room floor, ostensibly studying the effects of taxation on the corporate balance sheet. Actually, though, she had gone over the same paragraph three times without absorbing any of it.

Dan Morgan's sternly handsome features kept obliterating the printed page in front of her. Why hadn't he called her in and told her his decision? Or told John Turner, for that matter? Or acknowledged the message Lisa had left with Doris? In it she had told him of her decision to go along with the transfer, so why hadn't he called to gloat about his victory or—to be fair, and more likely—to thank her for cooperating?

"That's all right, don't get up," Marc grumbled, struggling to his feet when the second peal of the bell was also ignored by Lisa. He had dropped by with two bulging grocery bags of dirty laundry a couple of hours ago and had been lounging against a stack of vividly colored cushions, thumbing through a magazine while waiting for the dryer to stop. His hair still damp from the shower he had helped himself to earlier, he wore running shorts and a tank top.

Barefoot, he padded to the front door. The bell chimed yet again.

"Cool your jets, will ya?" he groused, yanking the door open with excessive force.

Dan Morgan frowned at the man in front of him, then down at the piece of paper in his hand. Apartment 209, it said, as did the number on the door this guy was holding open. This damp-haired, half-naked guy, Dan grimly added, deciding that calling first might have been a good idea.

"I'm looking for Lisa Hanrahan," he said stiffly.

"Yeah. And who're you?"

Unfriendly type, Dan thought, taking in the narrowed eyes and aggressive stance, the black curly hair on head and chest. Women probably liked him, though. They seemed to go for the wild pirate look this character had. Complete with earring.

The knowledge that Lisa was obviously part of that admiring throng of females brought an irrational stab of...disappointment. For the tenth time since leaving home, Dan asked himself why he had come.

"I'm Daniel Morgan," he introduced himself reluctantly, feeling none too friendly himself by then. "But never mind, I'll see Miss Hanrahan tomorrow."

Dan would have turned and left, but at the mention of his name, the guy's beard-shadowed cheeks dimpled in a blinding smile while he threw the door wide and grabbed Dan's arm.

"Hey, 'sokay. Come in," he said.

And then Lisa appeared, wide-eyed and disheveled, clad in a belted chenille robe and just as barefoot as her...companion.

"Mr. Morgan," she gasped, "what are you doing here?"

Dan was just asking himself the same question yet again and, unable to adequately answer it, cursed himself for an idiot. It was embarrassingly obvious that he had inter-

rupted an intimate evening, if their respective states of un-
dress and the rumpled piles of cushions littering the floor
behind them were any indication. And, as far as he was
concerned, they were.

"Look, I'm sorry," he said, trying without success not to
notice the way the fabric of Lisa's robe hugged her small but
curvy frame. "I shouldn't have come."

"Don't be silly," Lisa protested when he turned to leave.
Her friend continued to lounge against the doorjamb with
a knowing sort of grin. Dan felt a momentary urge to loosen
a few of those perfect teeth, when a small hand touched his
arm.

"Please come in," Lisa insisted, "now that you're here."

Dan allowed himself to be pulled inside and deeper into
what appeared to be the living room.

"Please sit down." Lisa pointed to one of the stacks of
cushions. "We don't have a lot of furniture yet, but those
are really quite comfortable. At least, we really like them,
don't we, Marc, and the good thing is, you don't have to
dust them." She gave a short, nervous laugh and rushed on.

"We're not too crazy about housework, are we, Marc,
even if we had the time to do it, which we don't. Why, it's
difficult enough to do the cooking, not that I'm very good
at that, either, and usually—"

"Lisa."

Lisa abruptly closed her mouth and snapped a look at
Marc, who made a sharp slicing motion across his throat
with his hand. He was telling her she'd been babbling, as she
always did when she was rattled and—boy, was she rattled
right now.

Daniel Morgan here, at her house, at this time of night.
What could he want? Was he planning to fire her after
hours, without witnesses? Of course not, silly, she told herself, and stifled a hysterical giggle, because he was sure
looking grim enough to do it.

She furtively darted another glance at Dan. He was standing in the middle of the room, frowning and looking kind of lost. Why, he's uncomfortable, too, she realized and immediately felt much calmer. Her manners asserted themselves.

"Mr. Morgan," she said, "may I introduce Marc Bennett. A very good friend," she added with a fond smile at the friend in question.

The men nodded curtly, Dan with a decided lack of cordiality, Marc with an air of bored curiosity.

"Why don't we sit down," Lisa invited again, doing so. She sensed that some inexplicable tension seemed to hover in the air and thought to diffuse it with social amenities. "Please, Mr. Morgan. Marc."

Dan lowered his long frame onto the pillows nearest him and folded his legs.

Marc remained standing. "I'll leave you two alone to talk," he said. "I'll be in the kitchen, Leece...."

Lisa felt a moment of unreasonable panic at the thought of being left alone with Daniel Morgan. She lifted her hand as if to detain Marc, but he was already gone. So she bent the extended arm and patted at her hair, pretending that that was what she had intended to do all along. Summoning what she hoped was a hostessy smile, she faced her guest.

Until then she hadn't had time to notice how different he looked tonight. In a charcoal sweater and chino pants, he was a far cry from the starchy executive in the suit. He still looked expensive, but seemed younger, less assured, more like some of the older students she knew. Lisa relaxed.

"So," she said brightly, "how have you been?"

"Fine, thank you."

"Doris gave you my message, I suppose?"

"Message?" Dan forced his attention away from the door through which that guy Bennett had disappeared and back to Lisa. "I'm sorry, I've been away at the Portland store...."

"Oh. I didn't know." Lisa waited for Dan to go on, to elaborate or to explain why he was here, but he said nothing, only looked preoccupied.

"Would you like some herbal tea?" she asked, hoping to bridge the pause that was quickly becoming awkward. "We have mint or—"

"No," Dan interrupted, adding a somewhat reluctant, "thank you," and jerkily running a hand through his hair.

"Look," he said, dropping the hand onto his knees. He stared down at it as if wondering where it had come from. "I'm sorry for barging in on you like this. I had no idea you...what I mean to say is, I came because I wanted to talk to you before another day went by, to tell you I've decided—oh, hell."

He looked up and glared at her accusingly. "Dammit, does that guy live here with you?"

"W-what?" Lisa gasped, caught completely off guard.

Incredibly Dan Morgan blushed. He looked away. "Forget it. It's none of my business."

"Well, no, it isn't," Lisa agreed. She was at a loss as to what to make of her employer's strange behavior. Did he think Marc...that she and Marc...? The half-formed notion seemed to her so ludicrous she wanted to laugh. But a quick glance at the thunderclouds wreathing Dan Morgan's face told her it would not be wise.

"On the other hand," she continued, "I really don't mind telling you that, no, Marc does not live here." She shrugged and gave a wry smile. "Though it seems as if he does, he's here so much."

"I see." Dan's tone made it clear he didn't much like that.

Lisa wondered at his attitude, would have liked to challenge it, but reminded herself of her vow not to rock any boats.

"His twin sister, Marcia, is my roommate," she explained. "Marc comes to eat, to do laundry, stuff like that."

"To shower?"

"Sometimes. He shares a small house with two other guys who tend to monopolize the premises." She shrugged again. "We're friends: Marc knows he's welcome here anytime."

"I see," Dan said again. He gave her an oddly searching glance before looking down at his hands. "And have you, uh, been friends long?"

"Seven years. Ever since I came to Seattle, just about. We met at The Mission."

"The Mission?"

"Downtown." Now it was Lisa's turn to dish out the searching glances. She eyed the superb fit of Dan's clothes, the heavy gold of his school ring, the buttery leather of his loafers. "I doubt you'd be familiar with the place. Your kind of people wouldn't hang out there."

His eyebrows raised at that. "And what kind of people would?"

"Poor people, Mr. Morgan. Homeless people. They are fed and sometimes sheltered there."

"And you . . . ?"

"I was one of those poor." Lisa met Dan's somber gaze with something like proud defiance in hers. He needn't think she was ashamed of who she was or that she was impressed by his obvious wealth.

"I'm fortunate in that I was never homeless. But I lived at The Mission for a while because I came from a large family and my father, who is a minister, couldn't afford to give me financial support when I left home. Our church is affiliated with The Mission, though, and Pop was able to get me room and board there in exchange for working around the place. I also did other odd jobs here and there."

Lisa shrugged. The gesture was meant to downplay the years of struggle. She detested self-aggrandizement of any kind, so she added, "After a while, what with my scholarships to the University of Washington and the money we saved, Marcia and I got this apartment."

"And Marc?"

"What about him?"

"Are you and he, uh, close?"

"Close?" Lisa wanted laugh again. Clearly Dan Morgan thought more than mere friendship bound her to Marc. It was heady, knowing it bothered him. Sort of exciting. And Lisa found she didn't want to tell him otherwise, nor to confess that between working and studying she had found neither time nor interest for men.

The doorbell rang.

"Excuse me, would you?" Lisa scrambled to her feet, glad not to have to give an answer, truthful or otherwise. After all, her affairs—or lack of them—were none of Daniel Morgan's business. She opened the door.

"Thanks, Leece, forgot my key." Marcia breezed inside, spied Dan, stopped and whistled long and low. "Lisa!" she exclaimed, sashaying toward Dan. "You little devil, you. Who is this yummy man?"

Lisa slammed the door and rushed back into the living room. Dan was getting up off his cushions while Marcia appreciatively watched his every move.

Lisa's elbow connected smartly with her friend's rib cage. "Marcia, honey, this is Daniel Morgan—my *employer*," she added in a meaningful tone. She sent Dan a bright smile. "Mr. Morgan, meet Marcia Bennett, my roommate."

"It's a pleasure to meet you, Miss Bennett."

"Marcia," she purred.

Dan took the hand she offered. "Marcia," he repeated politely. "I believe I met your, uh, twin brother, is it? Lisa's boyfriend?"

"Lisa's what?" Marcia nearly choked on a shriek of laughter. "Is that what you told this lovely man, Leece? Shame on you."

Lisa winced. She avoided Dan's gaze but could feel it drilling into her. She was looking daggers at Marcia, who was fluttering inch-long false lashes and saying, "She's such a tease, our Lisa. Why, we're all just friends here."

Lisa's elbow cut her short once again. "Good night, Marcia," she said. "Mr. Morgan and I have business to discuss."

"No hurry," Dan assured the women with a wide grin. "Just friends, huh?" He suddenly felt better than he had all night.

"Marcia's had a long day," Lisa said with teeth clenched. "Haven't you, Marcia?"

"No, I . . . oh!" Catching Lisa's eye and correctly inter-preting its glaring message at last, Marcia pulled her hand out of Dan's grip. "Yeah. Sure. I guess, I, uh—I'll see you around, Mr. Morgan." She pulled a face at Lisa. "Marc still here?"

"In the kitchen."

"Okay. Well, uh, good night." She winked at Daniel, dismissed Lisa's frown with a shrug and a toss of her sil-very mane and flounced from the room.

"Good night," Dan said before turning to Lisa and add-ing, deadpan, "Nice girl."

Lisa's reply came in the form of a garbled snort.

Dan pointed to the cushions. "Shall we sit again?"

"Well, actually—" At that point, Lisa just wanted him gone. Wouldn't you know the one time she tried to be a bit mysterious, she'd end up looking like an idiot? She glanced at her watch and saw she wasn't wearing it. "It's getting late," she finished lamely.

"I haven't told you why I came to see you yet." Dan's unexpected smile was tender. He caught her hand to keep her from moving away from him and looked down at it nestled in his. And he was more than a little surprised to note that though it was small, there was nothing childlike about it. It was a well-shaped and mature hand, a woman's hand—though perhaps a touch more work worn and capable than the female hands he was accustomed to holding.

A strong hand, he found as Lisa tugged to free it. He firmed his grip. "I'm sorry for prying into your personal life earlier," he said soberly. "I didn't mean to offend you, I merely wondered..."

What *had* he wondered, Dan asked himself, falling silent as he pondered that. The idea that Lisa Hanrahan might be...involved with a man had bothered him. More than bothered him, it had made him furious.

Bemused, Dan stared at the hand he was still holding. He turned it palm up and absently noted the well-established calluses there. At the sight of them, lined up like harsh monuments to the kind of labor no hand this size should have to do, he barely managed to stop himself from pressing a kiss onto each one of them.

He dropped her hand as if burned and took a step away from her. He cleared his throat.

"I've decided to keep you in security," he announced, harrumphing once again. "Though I, uh, intend to keep an eye on the department and, uh, on your performance." He briefly hesitated, then gave a short nod. "That's all I really came to say. Turner can fill you in on anything else."

He strode to the door, opened it, then turned and looked back at Lisa.

She stood where he had left her, in the middle of the cushion-strewn floor. His eyes were drawn to hers as if by magnets. Large, black, soft and liquid as those of a doe, they dominated her heart shaped face. Caught up in them, their very lack of guile beguiled him and their innate innocence oddly tempted.

Before he could completely forget himself and the principles he strove to honor, Dan muttered a curt good-night and fled.

Lisa stood where she was and stared at the apartment door. A myriad of odd, disquieting feelings assailed her, and though she had never experienced most of them before, she was widely read and could guess their identity.

What she did not feel, strangely, was triumphant. Shouldn't she be feeling that? she wondered. She had won the battle without a fight, hadn't she? Why did that seem so unimportant suddenly?

Much more important to her seemed the question of why, after years of closely working, associating and studying with some darned good-looking men, was she suddenly entertaining carnal fantasies about this particular one?

She could still feel the warmth of his hand cradling hers, and when he had stared into her palm—Lord, how she'd longed for him to kiss her there. She thought of his smile and had to smile, too. She closed her eyes and saw the tall, lean length of him, the narrow-hipped strength of him....

Good grief, girl, stop!

Lisa's eyes flew open. Heat suffused her face and body. She turned as if to run from the room but was stopped by the twins and their curious stares.

"Something wrong, Leece?"

"No, of course not." Lisa turned away and busied herself, tidying cushions to avoid their searching looks. "Da—Mr. Morgan came to tell my I'm staying in security."

"Super."

"So why don't you look happy?" Marc demanded. "Did the guy come on to you, or something?"

"No!" *As if he would.* That thought more than anything had her snapping upright and around, primed for a fight. "But what if he had—so what? Or maybe I came on to him, have you thought of that?"

She stormed from the room, completely missing the looks of shock Marc and Marcia exchanged.

Chapter Four

Dan couldn't sleep. He tossed and turned on his king-size water bed, causing a veritable tempest that at times threatened an untimely reversal of his evening meal. Or maybe it was something else that clutched at his innards and squeezed.

Worry? Yes, that was certainly part of it. The near fiasco with Lisa Hanrahan had hammered home to him the extent of his responsibilities as an employer. Hundreds of jobs, of human lives, of families, depended on him to make the kinds of decisions that would not jeopardize their financial security and future.

Dan conceded the victory of his boxing match with his pillow to the pillow—its lumps refused to budge. He got up off the bed. Maybe a glass of milk...

He padded naked and barefoot into the small kitchen. Not bothering to turn on the light, he found a glass, filled it and carried it back into the bedroom. Though it was still August, the night air chilled him. He grabbed the sheet off his bed, wrapped it around himself toga-style and went to stand by the window.

The lake below lay mirror still and mysterious in the moonlight. Across its silvery expanse the eastern shore was a black silhouette of houses and trees with only a patch of yellow light here and there to remind him that few were awake in the dead of night. He speculated fleetingly on the other insomniacs' pressing concerns, but his own turbulent thoughts were quick to override anything else.

Lisa Hanrahan. The name seemed never to be far from his consciousness these days. Even while his hands and his mind were occupied with other tasks, she hovered at the edge of awareness. Of course, they had had more confrontations in the course of their short acquaintance than some people had in years, which might explain it. On the other hand...

Dan sipped his milk, pensive, no longer consciously beholding the glittering lakescape below. He was marveling at how it was possible to only have known someone for a week yet feel as if she had always been a part of his life. An important part. He could not remember ever feeling such an...elemental connection to anyone before. Nor was he sure that he liked it or that, given their respective roles, the feeling was appropriate.

On his eighteenth birthday his grandfather, Jefferson Morgan, founder of the Morgan's Department Store chain, had called Dan into his study, poured him two fingers of bourbon whisky and said, "You're a man today, Danny, and a man needs to know certain things. One is how to hold his liquor. Drink up, boy."

Dan had obediently drained his glass, nearly expiring in the process as the smooth heat of the bourbon stole his breath and made him shudder.

Without a word, his grandfather had poured him another double. "The other has to do with women," he'd said, raising his own glass in a toast. "Here's to 'em!"

That time the stuff had gone down much more easily, and
the tingling languor that spread through his limbs and be-
fogged his brain had actually been quite pleasant. He'd held
out his glass for another round, and Grandad had been most
accommodating.

"Wonderful creatures, women," he had said, adding,
"but just like good bourbon, you partake of them spar-
ingly, boy. And you pick 'em out with care. I'm going to say
this once and I expect you to remember it: only a fool messes
around with the hired help, the skirts he works with, or his
best friend's sister. The first, because they'll start to boss
you, instead of the other way around. The second, because
it's counterproductive while it's going on and damned awkward when it's over. The third, because they'll expect you
to marry 'em...."

Dan had been sick as a dog after their little talk, but he
had never forgotten the points his grandfather had driven
home. Moderation in things pleasurable; discretion and
discrimination when choosing companions of the opposite
sex.

Dan neither indulged nor condoned romantic liaisons in
the workplace. But then, those nebulous feelings Lisa Hanrahan aroused in him had nothing to do with romance. Did
they?

Of course not!

Dan stretched in a noisy yawn and wearily rubbed the
stiffened muscles at the back of his neck. He moved away
from the window, set his empty glass on the nightstand and
unwrapped the sheet from around his body. He spread it
back on the bed. A little stiffly, he settled himself beneath
its coolness, yawned once more and sleepily picked up his
train of thought. His feelings for Miss Hanrahan were
merely philanthropic, he decided. After all, the Morgan
family had always been philanthropists. They established

scholarships and helped the needy—students and otherwise—in all sorts of ways.

Lisa Hanrahan was just one such needy student. According to Turner, a dress of hers had gotten ripped in a tussle
with a female shoplifter. Replacing it was the least he, Dan,
could do. The fact that he looked forward to seeing her in
something other than jeans and a T-shirt did not enter into
it at all.

Lisa had been at the store since it opened that morning.
She was scheduled to work six hours and, with three lab
hours at the university afterward, it would be one of her
longer days.

John had put her on "rubber checks," which meant te-
dious hours on the telephone, calling those customers whose
checks were returned to Morgan's for insufficient funds. It
was one of Lisa's least favorite assignments.

She had not seen Dan Morgan since he had come to her
apartment two nights ago. Not that there was any reason to
expect to see him, she hastened to assure herself, it was just
that he had more or less said he would be keeping his eye on
her....

She had not slept too well after he had left, the craziest
images and notions had popped into her head. And the
things she had caught herself feeling and wishing did not
bear thinking about in daylight. Yet think about them she
did, even as she absently entered columns of names, dates
and figures into a dog-eared journal.

The way his eyes turned almost silver when he smiled.
And the way her toes curled in reaction. The way her hand
was all but swallowed up in his when he had held it, how
good it had felt being held. The tingling in her veins, the
sweet melting sensation in the pit of her stomach...

So vivid were the images and feelings, it took Lisa a moment to realize that the ringing she was hearing through a

fog of dreamy introspection was, in fact, the telephone at her elbow.

"Security," she answered, and had to clear her throat and repeat the word to make it understandable.

"Miss Lisa Hanrahan, please." Lisa didn't recognize the female voice at the other end, but its no-nonsense tone dispelled the last of her fanciful imaginings.

"Speaking," she said every bit as crisply as her caller.

"Mr. Curt Dirkson, of Misotec, calling. One moment, while I put him on."

Almost immediately, Curt Dirkson was on the line. "Miss Hanrahan? How have you been? Say, would it be possible..."

Some five minutes later, when Lisa hung up, she was dazed but beaming. In her mind's eye the future sparkled with brightly illuminated dollar signs. Tomorrow she would sign a contract with Misotec, and at a fabulous salary.

Ecstatic, she hugged herself. To think that Mr. Misotec himself, C. A. Dirkson—call me Curt, he'd said—had practically *begged* her to sign on with his firm even before her master's was completed. And though he had said she could start work right away, he had understood that she wanted to stay at Morgan's until the three months she had promised John Turner were up.

They just wanted to be sure she wouldn't get away from them, he'd said. They needed people of her caliber. Her professors had spoken highly of her. Oh, boy, oh, boy—she couldn't wait to tell the twins....

By the time Lisa unlocked the door of the apartment later on that afternoon, some of the glow had dimmed. No wonder, she thought sourly, vigorously shaking her sopping umbrella out in the hall before leaning it against the door frame to let it drip. How could anyone keep the flame of happiness burning when buckets of rain were being dumped on it?

Shedding army surplus slicker and soggy sneakers, she squeaked into the living room on wet socks. Barely inside, she stopped. Hello, what was this?

Aside from the usual stacks of cushions, a large rectangular box and a yellow sheet of paper littered the floor, offending her sense of order. Lisa stepped closer and squinted down at Marcia's temperamental script.

"Toots, these came 4 U. The delivery person was real cute, but (sigh) too young. Just my luck. xxoo Marcia"

Lisa grinned and shook her head. A nut case, that girl. She laid the note aside and studied the parcel. For her? Never. Who would send her things from Kaiser & Fromm, that exclusive dress shop? Not the twins, they couldn't afford to—even if it was her birthday, which it was not.

Kneeling down, she carefully inspected the package. It was big. She leaned closer. Her name was inscribed on a little envelope attached to it. "Miss Lisa R. Hanrahan," it said.

Gingerly she picked up the box, expecting any moment to hear some strident voice call, "What are you doing? Put that down."

She weighed it, shook it. It wasn't heavy so much as awkward, and she couldn't feel anything move inside. She checked the envelope once more. It had her name on it, all right.

Lisa inhaled deeply. Surely it would be okay if she opened it.

Easing a finger beneath each strip of adhesive tape, taking care not to rip anything, she worked the wrapping off. Then she lifted the lid off the box, folded aside the layers of white and rustly tissue paper and gasped as something beautifully bright and silky was exposed.

Quickly, guiltily, Lisa folded the paper back down and picked up the lid to replace it ... only to put it aside again. What the heck, she rationalized, she had come this far.... What would it hurt to just take it out and look at it?

Carefully she peeled the tissue back again and there it was. A blouse or dress, she couldn't tell which, but there was no mistaking the designer label. Lisa pulled the garment out with shaking hands and held it aloft. It was a dress. Perfectly simple in its cut and style, the vivid print on a bright blue background gave it the kind of flash and dash Lisa loved. It was gorgeous.

Lovingly, taking care not to wrinkle anything, Lisa folded the dress back into the box. For the third time she checked the name. Who would send her such a dress?

A name suggested itself but was hastily discarded. He wouldn't, she thought, frowning darkly at the rumpled throw rug on which she knelt. Would he?

Her gaze skipped past the envelope still attached to the lid of the box before its significance sank in. She glanced sharply back. An envelope, dummy. No doubt with a note inside. She had it in her hand and was ripping it open without further thought. Her hands shook a little as she unfolded the crisp little card it contained. She acknowledged the embossed initials, D.J.M., with a tightening of her lips and scanned the brief message below. With an oath her father would not have approved of, she scrunched the card into a tight little ball in her fist.

"Daniel J. Morgan," she said, hurling the paper ball across the room. She jumped to her feet and with one well-placed kick sent the box flying after it. Then she immediately dropped back down onto her knees, grabbed the phone and furiously punched out the number for Morgan's Department Store. In jerky tones she asked the store operator for Mr. Morgan, Jr.

Doris came on the line and was sorry to say that Mr. Morgan had left for the day. Was there...

Lisa did not hear the rest. With a strangled thank-you, she slammed down the receiver and reached for the directory. Just lucky for him he was listed, she muttered fiercely as her rigid finger stabbed at the buttons again. One ring... two...let him be home. Five...six...

Damn, she thought, and swore again. Fleetingly it occurred to her that she had done more swearing since meeting that man than in her entire life before that.

After the eighth ring, she slammed the phone down again. Morgan was out. How could she stand not being able to tell him off? Humiliated pride all but choked her. She checked her watch. Lab in half an hour. Now what? No way was she keeping this...this *handout* here overnight.

Her mind made up, Lisa copied down Dan's address and gathered up the dress and package, which had parted company in the course of her kick. She folded the garment carefully once again and secured the lid with tape.

Rushing into her bedroom, she scooped up her books, stuffed them into the backpack and, on the way out the door, slipped into rubber boots and a camouflage-patterned slicker. Moments later, with her pack across one shoulder and the dress box balanced awkwardly against her chest, she stepped out into the pouring rain and sloshed toward the bus stop.

Several unproductive hours of lab time later, an infinitely soggy Lisa was at the massive plate-glass doors of the Marine View Manor. In the entry, marble and brass gleamed, bespeaking the well-heeled exclusivity of the building's inhabitants. This splendor was a far cry from the peeling walls and banged-up, sagging doors of Lisa's building's entrance, but then that was hardly surprising. Hers was a world of have-nots, while this was how the haves were accustomed to living.

With a disparaging snort Lisa rang the bell beneath the sign stating 532—Morgan. A faint crackle issued from the intercom, and then Dan's voice.

"Yes, hello?"

"It's Lisa Hanrahan."

If Dan was surprised by her almost surly tone or, indeed, by the fact that she was there at all, he gave no indication of it. "I'll buzz you in," he answered calmly.

The first thing Lisa saw as she emerged from the elevator with the rapidly disintegrating box in her arms, was Dan Morgan lounging in his doorway. To see him standing there so casually, so obviously warm and dry in chinos and a V-necked sweater and so plainly amused at her own sodden state, was almost enough to make her turn around and leave. Almost.

With as much dignity as her noisily squishing rubber boots and drooping burden allowed, Lisa marched up to Dan and halted about a foot in front of him.

"Here," she pronounced, jiggling her arms to indicate that she meant for him to relieve her of the parcel. "This is yours, I believe."

Dan's brows lifted and his grin expanded into a smile of such warmth that Lisa was hard put to ignore it. "Actually," he said mildly, "I meant it to be yours. What's the problem, wrong size?"

"No. Wrong woman. I do not accept—"

"Why don't we discuss it inside?"

"I have no intention of coming in. What I have to say won't take but a moment. Mr. Morgan—"

"Dan," he interjected.

"Mr. Morgan—" Lisa broke off because her arms were aching from the strain of holding the box. "If you don't take this from me, I'm going to drop it on the spot."

Dan hastened to take the package from her.

"I only came to say that I do not accept charity under any circumstances," she informed his averted back. "Thank you, and good night." She turned to leave.

Tossing the box into the apartment, Dan spun around and captured her arm. "Charity?" he exclaimed. "What are you talking about?"

"I'm talking about being capable of buying my own clothes, thank you very much." She yanked her arm out of his hold, but Dan immediately caught her again.

"Not so fast." He reached to catch the other arm, too. "Since you're here, I insist you come in and warm up. You owe me a proper explanation, at least."

"I owe you nothing but an honest day's work." Lisa fought to resist the gentle tug of his hands and the much more subtle yet compelling beckoning of his eyes. She had done what she had come to do, the sooner she got out of there, the better.

"Come on," Dan coaxed, already moving backward with her in tow.

"No, really, I..." She threw a last, almost desperate look toward the elevator as Dan relentlessly drew her into his apartment. "Well, maybe just for a little while," she muttered, and for her own peace of mind added a silent, *Just to be polite*.

Once inside, Dan's hands immediately went to tug the backpack off her shoulders and the slicker up over her head.

"You're soaked," he chided, "don't you have an umbrella? Let's get those boots off. How the heck did you get here, walk?"

"Yes." Lisa felt ridiculously choked up at his fussing, and consequently the tone of her affirmative reply was anything but cordial. If it hadn't been for *him*, she wouldn't be so wet.

Dan seemed oblivious to the negative vibrations she tried to give off. He was all business, down on his knees, pulling off her sodden socks.

"Your boots leak," he scolded. "Don't you own anything that doesn't have holes in it? And did you have to wade through every puddle on your way over here? Where'd you come from, anyway, the other side of the lake? *Through the damn lake?*"

A giggle threatened to sneak past Lisa's tightly compressed lips and was hastily swallowed. Still, she couldn't help but smile as she thought, *If only John Turner could see us now....*

Dan had gotten a towel and was briskly rubbing her feet, making her lift first one leg and then the other. For balance, she was clutching a shoulder that felt reassuringly solid through the down soft wool of his sweater. Cashmere, she noted. Naturally. She relaxed her grip and allowed one finger to stroke the velvety texture.

One of these days, she promised herself. Just as soon as she was working for Misotec...

Misotec. The name abruptly snatched her from her foolish reverie. What on earth was she doing mooning over sweaters the price of which could feed a family for a month? And, as if that wasn't bad enough, with her foot in the hands of the kind of man who probably never gave such matters a thought.

She yanked her foot out of Dan's hands.

"I came here from the university," she said in reply to his question. "And now I've really got to be going." She bent to wrestle the socks from his hands. "I shouldn't be here like this, it's—"

"Relax, Lisa." Dan won the battle of the socks. "Just let me toss these into the dryer."

"No. I mean, they'll only get wet again and anyway, I just wanted to return the package and tell you—"

"I know—you don't accept charity. Forget that for a moment, will you? Let's get you warmed up."

Ignoring her spluttered protest, he propelled her into the living room where a cheery fire crackled in the hearth. Its lure was impossible to resist and Lisa gave up trying. She dug her frozen toes into the warm and cushy carpet and glanced around at the quietly luxurious furnishings.

It was a struggle not to be intimidated by the understated evidence of wealth. Or impressed.

Abstract pictures in deceptively simple frames hung here and there, and though Lisa would not have been able to identify any of them, she knew instinctively they were neither prints nor copies. What wooden furnishings there were—a sideboard, some bookshelves, a coffee table—were simply styled and darkly gleaming.

Mahogany perhaps, Lisa thought, the solid kind, not veneer. And a far cry from rickety rattan and stacks of cheap pillows. She stood rooted where Dan had left her. Uncomfortable. Resentful.

To date, the home of Mayor Schulberg back in Pineville had been the most opulent house she had ever been in—and then only to help with the cleaning. She had thought it a castle, but not even he had lived as finely as this, and he was the owner of the largest lumber mill around.

Lisa thought of Isabelle Schulberg, the mayor's daughter, and shuddered, remembering the girl's snickers and whispers whenever she had seen Lisa in one of her hand-me-down dresses.

Charity, Lisa thought bitterly—what was it to people like the Schulbergs but the giving away of things they no longer wanted so that they could feel superior.

She chafed her arms against a sudden chill and reminded herself that she was light-years away from Pineville and those unpleasant memories.

She watched Dan bustle around, plumping cushions on the sofa. "You have a beautiful home," she told him.

"Really?" He straightened to look at her, brows raised, lips quirked in a quizzical smile. "So why the fierce frown?"

"Was I frowning?" Lisa concentrated on smoothing her brow. "I didn't mean to."

"Just as you didn't mean the disapproving tone in which you voiced the compliment?" Dan took a few steps until he stood in front of her. It was his turn to frown as he peered down into her face. "Why don't you tell me how you really feel about my home, Lisa."

"It's lovely. I told you." She wouldn't meet his gaze.

"But..." Dan prompted, lifting her chin with one long finger and forcing her to look at him. "I hear a gigantic *but* in your voice." He searched her face, stubbornly shuttered. "Well?"

"All right, I'll tell you." Lisa knew further prevarication would be pointless. Dan Morgan was determined to make her talk, but he wasn't going to like what she had to say.

"I think it's sinful for one person to live like this while others barely live at all. I'm wondering how it is you don't feel guilty about that, Mr. Morgan."

"What makes you think I don't?"

"Well, I assumed..." Lisa blinked, taken aback, then rallied. "Do you?"

"No." Dan's expression had hardened, but it held no apology. He straightened, but kept his eyes on Lisa's. "I've worked for everything you see in this apartment, Miss Hanrahan. And everything my family owns has been acquired through my father's and grandfather's business acumen and tireless dedication. Thanks to their efforts Morgan's employs many hundreds of people, and supports a great many charities—"

"With money." Lisa all but spat the word.

"You have something against money, Miss Hanrahan?" Dan's tone was silken.

"I have when it's used as a panacea for every ill, yes. Money isn't the answer to every problem, Mr. Morgan. There are people out there who need more than cash, more than handouts. People who need someone to talk to, a human touch, a *real* helping hand—"

"Such as you are giving at The Mission?"

Lisa blinked again, disconcerted for the second time by one of Dan's mild interjections. "Well...yes," she mumbled, suddenly out of steam and shivering again. "Something like that."

"You're cold." Dan thought Lisa's opinions intriguing, and one of these days he would have to challenge her on them, but what she needed right now was to be wrapped in a blanket and warmed up. He caught her by the arm and hustled her toward the sofa facing the fire.

"Sit," he ordered, pushing her down on it. "And stay."

Lisa felt like telling him she was not a dog to be ordered around, but Dan had already left the room. He returned in the blink of an eye, carrying a blanket. Without ceremony he bent and grabbed her legs, swung them onto the couch and covered them and her with the blanket.

"I'll be right back," he said, and left again before Lisa could reply, much less protest. She hesitated only briefly, then cautiously let her head fall back against the arm of the couch. If she stayed and enjoyed this for just a few minutes, she rationalized, what could be the harm? Wiggling her toes beneath the soft wool of the blanket, she let a small sigh escape. She closed her eyes, bemused and unnerved by the host of strange feelings creeping in. Feelings of rightness, almost of contentment.

Just for a moment she would put aside her unease. Just for a little while she would indulge herself and the fantasy that this was her home. More, that the man who was so incongruously doing his best to pamper her was the one with whom she shared it.

Stretching her legs and scooting further down under the blanket, Lisa soaked up the peaceful atmosphere like a flower soaks up sunshine. This was so nice. This was just as she had always imagined sitting by a fire would be. The faint smell of smoke, the crackling of the burning logs, the special kind of warmth that central heating just could not provide. And Dan—

Preceded by the pungent aroma of hot mulled wine, the man she had been about to romanticize walked back into the living room. Lisa quickly popped upright and opened her eyes, profoundly glad that thoughts were invisible.

"This is just the thing for you," he proclaimed, bending to help wrap her hands securely around the mug. "Careful, though, it's hot."

So was the touch of his hands on hers. Lisa worked hard to concentrate on the aroma of cloves and cinnamon that tantalized her nostrils as she took a cautious sip. "Hmm," she murmured, blowing at the steamy brew before sipping once more. "Delicious. Thank you."

Dan stood and watched her with an expression of pleased indulgence, and Lisa felt herself warmed by the look as much as by the drink and the fire. For a moment their gazes clung, and the crackle in the air between them had nothing to do with the logs on the grate.

Lisa blinked. She quickly looked away.

Dan cleared his throat. "I was just going to fix myself some dinner," he said. "Have you eaten?"

Before Lisa could voice an untruthful yes, her stomach grumbled its own very audible answer. Embarrassed, she shot Dan a pink-faced glare as if daring him to comment.

Dan grinned, but only said, "That settles it, I think. How does the specialty of the house sound to you, hmm? Broiled steak Daniel and tossed salad Maria."

Charmed by his relaxed and easy manner but still not at all sure that staying was a good idea, Lisa asked, "Who's Maria?"

"My housekeeper. She prepared the salad before she left. It's way too much for me and I detest eating alone."

Lisa was tempted. She was so comfortable. He was so nice. What could be the harm? And steak... Steak was not something she and Marcia could afford very often.

"Well..." Hunger beat out the last of her reservations. "Steak and salad sounds terrific," she admitted with a smile. "I'll help, of course."

"No way." Dan forestalled her move off the couch. "I'll be back before you know it."

And he was.

Dan placed a small card table near the fireplace and covered it with a white cloth that matched the snowy monogrammed napkins. Real linen, Lisa noted, the kind of stuff that somebody had to carefully launder and iron. Knowing *that* somebody was not likely to be Dan, Lisa took care not to soil the cloth.

Dinner was delicious. Filet mignon, sauteed mushrooms, tossed salad and crusty hot sourdough bread. Lisa savored every bite. Throughout the meal Dan kept up a stream of light conversation which, along with the wine, soon loosened Lisa's tongue, as well.

They swapped college stories, finding that they had quite a few experiences in common. Dan too had attended the University of Washington School of Business, though he had gotten his M.B.A. at Harvard. Still, being fellow alumni allowed them to share a laugh at the expense of some bumbling professors they had both known and to exchange pet peeves with perfect understanding.

Dan told Lisa of his family and how every Sunday he was expected to dine at the home of his parents.

"As far as my mother is concerned, only serious ill-ness—and I'm talking deathbed here—or a trip out of town, are acceptable excuses for absence."

They both laughed. Lisa had been listening with great interest to his recital, thinking that his parents sounded very much like her own. She had met his father, of course, and had liked him, as did most of the staff at Morgan's. He was one of those old-school executives who made it a point to know his employees personally.

Mrs. Morgan had once been pointed out to Lisa on one of the lady's infrequent visits to the store. She had seemed rather cold, very elegant and regal, without any trace of her husband's warm expansiveness. Now, listening to Dan, it became clear to Lisa that she had obviously been wrong in her assessment. Just as she had been wrong in thinking Dan Morgan a stuffed shirt?

"But what about you?" Dan asked, snapping Lisa out of her contemplation of the pitfalls of first impressions. "I know you mentioned once that yours was a very large family. Just how large is large?"

"How does nine older brothers strike you?"

Dan laughed. "Large," he said with great emphasis, suitably impressed. "And your father is a minister. Where abouts?"

"In, uh, Pineville. That's a small town, east of the mountains," Lisa replied. "Unfortunately, I can rarely afford to visit them more than once a year."

As she talked, she fidgeted, no longer at ease. Mention of her father had brought to mind the standards of conduct that had always been expected of her. To sit drinking wine, barefoot and unchaperoned, in a bachelor's apartment was breaking every one of his rules.

Watch and pray that you may not enter into tempa-tion.... She could all but hear her father recite the words of Mark. Was this temptation?

She glanced over at Dan and, catching an unguarded, almost predatory look in the intense brightness of his eyes, knew that it was. Still she was powerless to pull her gaze from his, and a rush of heat, a melting sort of ache, made her insides quiver. Made her long to seek his closeness, to touch and be touched. To love and be—

Good Lord, what was she thinking?

"I've got to go!"

Lisa was on her feet and practically bolting from the room when Dan caught her wrist and stopped her. He cupped her shoulder and slowly turned her around until they were facing each other.

"You haven't told me why you don't want the dress," he said softly, one finger beneath her chin and urging it upward.

The dress. Lisa flushed scarlet. How could she have forgotten the very thing that had brought her here in the first place? The answer immediately presented itself. She had let Dan Morgan and his polished charm momentarily seduce her.

"Let go of me," she said, furious with herself and with Dan for her lapse.

"Not until you tell me—"

"I don't take charity."

"So you've said. The dress, however, is restitution, not charity."

"I don't want it."

"Turner said your dress got torn on duty—"

"I don't want it," she repeated, the fire in her eyes daring him to pursue the subject.

Dan seemed about to argue further, but sighed instead. He stared at her, his gaze turning dark. "Do you know what I want?" he asked in a husky voice.

"N-no..." Dan's eyes on her lips were hot as the sun. Lisa licked at a sudden dryness. And then, light-headed from the unaccustomed wine and dizzy from the equally unaccustomed longings that swept her, she raised herself on tiptoe and, as if mesmerized, waited as Dan dipped his head and slowly, slowly, lowered his mouth to hers.

Their lips touched with all the spark and sizzle of two hot wires fusing. Jolted clear down to her toes, Lisa took hold of the arms that were pulling her boneless body against the solidity of his and clung. Shivers of reaction, of fevered excitement, raced through her as she felt his tongue caress her lips, probe at her teeth.

Instinctively she relaxed and welcomed him into a part of her she had never shared with anyone before. So this was how it felt to want, she thought dreamily, pressing closer. So good, so right—

Wrong! This is wrong! The words sundered the sultry haze in which she drifted. Lisa froze. She jerked out of Dan's embrace, hooked a foot around one of his calves and, with the speed and ease that comes from years of practice, flipped Daniel Morgan smartly onto his backside.

Chapter Five

Dan sat a moment, stunned. He wasn't sure what had transpired. All he knew was that one moment he had been savoring the softest pair of lips this side of heaven, and the next his butt had connected painfully with the hardest damn floor this side of Hades. And facing him, wild-eyed and disheveled, was Lisa Hanrahan.

"Kung fu?" he managed to croak.

Lisa shook her head, slowly retreating. "Brothers," she gasped before she whirled and bolted from the room. She wanted only to get away, away from temptation and the dangerous feelings Dan Morgan had aroused with just one kiss.

And away from the wrath that was sure to erupt just as soon as he gathered his wits and got up off the floor.

She had flipped Dan Morgan, Lisa marveled, stifling a hysterical urge to giggle. She had tossed him as if he were no more than just another of the would-be Casanovas she had similarly dealt with over the years. Of course, he had asked for it—he shouldn't have kissed her!

And you, you idiot, shouldn't have come here. Worse, you shouldn't have stayed.

Lisa struggled furiously to get her foot into the damp boot, calling herself all kinds of a fool. When Dan spoke from behind her, she promptly lost her balance and sat down on the floor with a thud.

Dan's look seemed to say tit for tat, but aloud all he said was, "I think these'll help." He extended her dried pair of socks.

"Thanks." Lisa tried to snatch them out of his hand, not daring to meet his eyes just then. He moved them out of reach until she looked up.

"I deserved that tumble," he told her soberly, then added with a tiny twinkle, "and I apologize for ever doubting your ability to defend yourself."

He gave her the socks. There followed a long pause during which their gazes remained on each other, and some undefinable aspect of their relationship subtly shifted and found a new niche.

"Thank you," Lisa said at last, her voice soft. And they both knew she didn't just mean for the socks.

"Will you trust me to drive you home?" Dan handed her the slicker.

Lisa's quiet yes came without hesitation.

If Lisa had expected to see any kind of change in her relationship with Dan Morgan after that night, she would have been disappointed. As it was, she was relieved that he acted as if they had never shared a single kiss or confidence between them—or so she told herself.

Dan was all business, and of course she would have been too had the occasion demanded it. As it was, it didn't. The only purpose of Dan's frequent visits to the security office seemed to be conferences with John Turner, and if Dan acknowledged her at all, it was with a casual wave or an equally casual, "Hi, there."

Yet every night she tossed restlessly on her solitary futon and relived each moment of their evening together in his apartment. And every night the memory of their little kiss expanded until it became a full-fledged scene of passion that stopped just short of completion only because her knowledge of *that* was limited to the mechanics gleaned from biology texts. There had never been the time nor the inclination to expand on theoretical knowledge before, but now...

She knew it was madness. It was crazy, stupid, to imagine herself doing intimate things with Dan Morgan, of all people. He was her employer, for heaven's sake. And while that fact could never make her want him, what it definitely should do was make her *not* want him.

Workplace romances were so tacky. How often had she watched them between some of the younger part-time members of the sales staff? Soulful glances across the hosiery, sweaty touches behind the display of jogging shoes... And when it was over, the hostility between the erstwhile lovers invariably affected their performance on the job.

Of course, she wouldn't be working at Morgan's all that much longer. She had had lunch with Curt Dirkson just days before and officially signed on with Misotec....

Stop it!

Lisa forced herself to focus on the monitor in front of her. At the moment she was still employed by Morgan's and had a job to do. The videotape she had been sightlessly staring at needed to be reviewed for court tomorrow morning, and she had notes to take, as well. Some witness she would make in her present state.

She prided herself on her arrest record, but she also wanted to see every shoplifter successfully prosecuted. Not only in civil court, where the store was generally awarded the price of the stolen merchandise plus restitution, but in criminal court, too. It was the only way to stop a crime that robbed not only businesses but, by virtue of higher prices, every consumer as well.

Grimly Lisa rewound the tape and watched again as the young woman on film stuffed a sleeveless summer dress into the bag attached to her toddler's stroller. The child was sleeping, blissfully unaware of Mom's criminal activities.

Lisa sighed, remembering the case. The woman had become hysterical when confronted outside the store, claiming somebody else must have put the dress there when she hadn't been looking. She had never stolen before, had never been in trouble.

Three aliases and a list of priors later, hysterics had given way to abuse. Lousy cops, rotten pigs, your mother...

Lisa had shrugged the insults off. After all, she knew what her own mother really was—a saint. A martyr to her family and her husband's congregation. A woman who had sacrificed her youth and her autonomy for the man she married. Never, never would Lisa similarly sacrifice her goals for a man.

Finished with the review, the tape rewound and put away, Lisa stood up. After placing the file and her notes into a filing cabinet, she picked up her purse and walked over to bid Terry, the part-time agent on duty with her, good-night.

He was watching the almost deserted sales floors on the regular monitors. It was five-thirty on a rainy Wednesday night. Not many shoppers lingered downtown on a night like this unless some major holiday was imminent.

"I hate to deprive you of my stimulating company, old buddy," Lisa said with a grin, "but I'm off."

"Stimulating company, my asparagus." Terry looked at her with undisguised displeasure. "Lately, you've been about as much fun as my calculus prof when he expounds on exponential equations. Go already, it can only cheer me up."

Lisa felt bad. She had been too preoccupied with personal thoughts to enjoy the customary lighthearted banter with her colleagues, most of whom were fellow students. Blast Dan Morgan anyway, she fumed, it was all his fault.

With a mumbled good-night, she walked out the door and straight into Dan Morgan's chest.

"Whoops," he said, his arms closing around her to steady her.

"Well put," Lisa snapped, glad to have a valid target on which to vent her temper. "Excuse me." She removed one of Dan's arms and, with a toss of her perpetually tousled mane, shouldered past him.

"Just a minute, Miss Hanrahan," Dan said quietly but with a hint of steel that stopped Lisa in her tracks.

Still she took her time turning to face him. "Yes, *sir*?"

Dan looked around and saw several pairs of eyes trained on them. He smiled politely and took Lisa's arm in a vise-like grip that made her wince. His grip loosened just a fraction.

"Let's step into the office, shall we," he said, and propelled her back through the door into the room she had just exited.

"Is this going to take long?" Lisa inquired, incensed by the way he was manhandling her. "If so—"

"Don't you dare," Dan warned, steering her past Terry into the larger room beyond. "Don't you dare start that spiel with the overtime again."

Remembering the other time she had used that ploy, Lisa couldn't keep from grinning. She slanted Dan a sidelong glance and saw glints of humor in the azure brightness of his eyes, too.

They stopped just inside the door. As one they turned to face each other, to silently regard each other. And their smiles slowly faded.

Dan's warming gaze shifted from Lisa's eyes to her mouth and lingered there like a lover's kiss. Her pulse began to race.

Immediately chagrined by her errant emotions, Lisa flushed furiously. She twisted out of his now gentle grip, and couldn't quite stifle a startled gasp. "Oh. John."

"Lisa." John Turner rose from behind the corner desk. His eyes darted from Lisa's flushed countenance to Dan Morgan's bland one. "Mr. Morgan."

"Ah, there you are, Turner," Dan said smoothly. "I'm glad we found you here. I was just going to tell Miss Hanrahan about tomorrow. Why don't you take care of it, instead, hmm?"

He turned to leave but stopped when John said, "What about that other thing? Anchorage—"

"No. Hold off on that. I'm still considering the pros and cons." He inclined his head toward Lisa. "Good night, Miss Hanrahan. I'll come by in the morning and pick you up."

As the door closed behind him, Lisa turned back to John. "What was he talking about, pick me up? I'm in court in the morning."

John nodded. "And so is he."

Lisa dressed for court in her job-interview outfit. She had bought it for her meetings with Misotec, realizing that a certain amount of conventionality was mandatory for a professional person lunching with her future employer.

Today, Lisa decided, the navy blue worsted wool suit and simple white blouse that would have done a nanny proud, would serve to impress her present employer, too. Not that she would care if it didn't, of course.

Promptly at eight, she opened the door in answer to Dan's ring. "Well," was all he seemed able to say at the sight of her, though his eyes spoke eloquently, indeed.

Lisa beamed, gratified and at ease enough to tease him. "You have such a way with words, Mr. Morgan. Am I to assume that you approve of my appearance for once?"

"Yes, Miss Hanrahan, you may assume so. Shall we?"

Dan stepped aside to let Lisa by, reaching past her to pull the apartment door shut just as she was abreast of him. His move abruptly brought them into intimate contact. Dan jerked his arm out of the way and smiled an apology.

Lisa flushed but managed what she hoped was a composed facade though her breast tingled from the inadvertent touch of his arm.

The hall and stairway of the old building were narrow, and they were forced to walk single file, with Lisa in the lead. She could feel Dan's eyes on her and, in spite of her feigned nonchalance, was ridiculously pleased with the knowledge that approval and admiration would be reflected in them.

On the short drive to the courthouse, Lisa briefly explained the particulars of the case, as well as her own strong feelings about it. Dan listened attentively.

She turned slightly in her seat and looked at him. As always, in his business suits and crisp shirts, Dan Morgan was an impressive and even intimidating sight.

"Why are you coming with me this morning?" she asked. John had not been very illuminating when she'd asked him the same thing.

Dan cast her a brief look. "To learn, of course."

"Surely you've been to court before, Mr. Morgan. I mean, everybody—"

"Everybody, Miss Hanrahan? What has brought you into court besides shoplifting cases for Morgan's?"

"Why, nothing, of course. I mean—"

"Right," Dan said dryly. "And the same is true for me. Not even so much as a traffic ticket. And since I intend to know every phase of every department in my store, I'm going along with you this morning to learn."

Parking in the underground facility, they took an elevator up to the floor on which their assigned courtroom was located. They'd agreed to leave the VCR they had brought to show the incriminating videotape in the car for the moment; Dan would fetch it when necessary.

They settled on one of the pewlike benches in the crowded courtroom, adding their own whispered exchanges to the general hum of conversation. All around them were groups of two or three people, conferring with their heads together, making notations on notepads, riffling through copious files. Lisa looked around to see if Angela Carson, their suspect, was in the room, but didn't see her.

"Is there a Lisa Hanrahan in the room?"

Lisa looked at the bespectacled young man standing near the front of the room, scanning it. She rose and approached him. "Good morning."

"Miss, ah, Hanrahan?" At Lisa's nod, he held out a limp hand. "I'm Carstairs Downing, Assistant City Attorney."

Lisa briefly shook his hand, barely controlling the urge to really squeeze it hard. She liked a firm clasp, but then that was neither here nor there at the moment. "Yes, Mr. Downing?" she inquired politely.

"I, ah, just wanted to make your acquaintance before the proceedings begin in, ah, three minutes or so," Downing said. "Of course, there's no telling at what time our case will come up, but it looks, ah, like a solid one for us. Scott Atherton will be acting as public defender for, ah, Ms., ah," he searched his notes for the defendant's name.

"Carson," Lisa helpfully supplied, thinking that, for an attorney, Mr. Downing was a depressingly cumbersome speaker.

She listened with barely leashed impatience while he outlined his intended prosecution in painstaking and boring detail.

"Please rise." The stentorian voice of the bailiff cut short the city attorney's monologue, and Lisa gratefully escaped back to her seat.

". . . now in session. The Honorable Horace K. Oxsmith presiding."

As Judge Oxsmith took his seat behind the raised bench, Lisa whispered a condensed account of her meeting with Downing into Dan's ear. A couple of times her lips lightly brushed the velvet of his lobe as she spoke, causing ripples of reaction to spread through her body. As soon as she could, without being obvious she straightened, striving to ignore her galloping pulse, as well as the warm gleam in Dan's eye.

The court calendar was being read and discussed between the judge and the various attorneys and prosecutors, but Dan and Lisa were often oblivious. Their senses were keenly attuned to each other and carried on an inaudible dialogue that had nothing to do with legal matters.

Lisa came to attention when *City of Seattle v. Angela Carson* was called. Carstairs Downing was responding to the effect that the city was ready to proceed.

An elderly rotund little man bounded to his feet. "If Your Honor please."

"Yes, Mr. Atherton?"

"Your Honor, defense would like to request a two-week continuance. There are a few more details, witnesses . . ."

Mr. Atherton went on to list his reasons, the judge granted postponement and, disgusted, Lisa stopped listening. She turned to Dan, who looked perplexed.

"Unless you want to stick around as a general spectator, Mr. Morgan, we might as well get out of here." Lord, but she resented these postponements and the waste of time. Not waiting for Dan's reply, she stood and marched out.

Dan followed more sedately, catching up with her in the hall. "What was that all about?" he asked.

"That, Mr. Morgan, was the justice mill at work," Lisa responded with a frown still crinkling the smoothness of her brow. "As you saw, it tends to grind exceedingly slowly."

She glared up at Dan as if he were at fault, but at his comically raised brows couldn't repress a rueful smile.

"Don't mind me," she said with a self-deprecating shake of the head. "I just get so darn frustrated. Three months ago the woman helps herself to a dress in our store. The evidence is right here." She lifted the slim briefcase containing the dress, videotape and file and shook it. "We finally get to court and what happens? Postponement. I hate that. I hate the way these things drag out."

Dan seemed to understand. He took her elbow and steered her into an empty elevator. "I think it's because you got yourself all steamed up to see justice done, were primed to testify and then—zip, all that steam for nothing. It's a letdown. But surely, this isn't the first time it's happened to you?"

"No, of course not. It seems to happen more often than not, that's just it. But I don't have to like it, do I?"

"No, you don't. So—how about I buy you lunch by way of compensation?"

Lisa laughed in spite of her ire. "It's nine-thirty in the morning."

"Breakfast, then."

"I've eaten, thanks."

"I haven't. Join me for coffee."

Lisa shook her head. "We, sir, are on company time here. They'll have our jobs if we're caught playing hooky in some restaurant."

Dan leaned closer. "I happen to have an in with the boss," he whispered with a conspiratorial wink and a poke in the ribs. "If he finds out, I'll fix it."

"Oh, yeah?" Lisa drawled. "What kind of an in?"

"I'll never tell." Dan laughed and held the door so Lisa could exit from the elevator. "So what do you say? Coffee?"

Lisa assented, as she had wanted to all along. They would only talk business, she assured herself.

As it turned out, they did. Dan had a lot of questions regarding security and was openly impressed by the extent of Lisa's knowledge.

More evidence of the colossal blunder he had made in his initial assessment of her, he ruefully admitted to himself. He had taken one look at the petite young woman in those ratty clothes and made up his mind that she would not do. So far, she had been doing pretty well in proving him wrong.

John Turner, however, was right. Lisa Hanrahan *was* the logical person to assist him with that mess in Anchorage.

He put it to her.

Lisa was taken aback at first. "The new Anchorage store?" she said, frowning. "Employee theft? Good Lord."

She stared at him, mulling over what he had said. "Why me?" she burst out after a lengthy silence, adding, "And *you*, of all people? Why not another security agent? Or, for that matter, why isn't Anchorage security handling it themselves?"

Dan sipped from his coffee, looking at her over the rim of his cup. "You, because outside of John you're the most experienced agent we have. Also, the best," he added after a short hesitation. He sipped again in silence.

He expected Lisa to preen, to at least don a look that said, *Isn't that what I told you?* But she did neither. She only looked at him with disconcerting directness and waited for the rest of what he had to say.

He set down his cup and cleared his throat.

"Me, for several reasons," he told her, ticking them off on his fingers. "One, my face is unknown to the people at the Anchorage store, having just come aboard the Morgan ship, as it were. Two, my father and the board of directors have put me in charge of bringing security for all our stores into the space age. Call it a special assignment that's independent of my appointment as manager of the Seattle store. And three—" He thought a moment and chuckled. "I guess there isn't a three."

Folding his arms and resting his elbows on the edge of the table, he leaned toward Lisa. "We'll both be undercover in this. I'll be an agent on loan from the Seattle store, assigned to observe and ostensibly to train the very inexperienced people they have up there. You, on the other hand, won't be security at all—officially. You'll have been hired to work in the warehouse. Here's how we thought things would go...."

Lisa listened attentively as Dan outlined what her duties in the warehouse would be, the general procedure there, etc. A part of her was intrigued by the challenge and the adventure of what he proposed, yet another part was apprehensive—for strictly personal reasons.

Two weeks in an alien environment. And with Dan Morgan the only person she knew. Two weeks of working closely with him, of being with him practically around the clock. The prospect was as frightening as it was tempting.

"If things go as planned, I might ask you to work with me on future security matters, as well," Dan said in closing. "The question right now is, can you take the time away from your studies for this? I know how far you've come and how important it is for you to finish in a timely fashion."

Not quite, you don't, Lisa thought, and felt a keen pang of conscience. Was she being fair in not informing Dan of her contract with Misotec? Shouldn't he be made aware that her time with Morgan's was drawing to an end?

She stared blindly down into her coffee cup, gnawing at her lower lip in an agony of indecision. If she told him, the assignment in Anchorage would be off—he would take someone else. The thought brought an odd stab of pain. She wanted very badly to go, suddenly. Badly enough to ignore the clamoring voice of her conscience and to smile at him brightly.

"I don't think my studies would be a problem," she said, adding with a chuckle, "The bummer will be telling Marc and Marcia that I'm taking a trip with you."

"Marc and Marcia?" Dan's eyebrows shot up. "Why on earth would they care?"

Lisa gave a rueful shrug, thinking of the dim view the twins took of anything to do with Dan Morgan. Ever since he had come to the apartment that night several weeks ago, they had watched Lisa like a pair of private eyes. They had noted her too-often dreamy state and most volubly laid the blame for that and for her new and uncharacteristic bouts of moodiness squarely at his feet.

"Sometimes they forget I'm a grown woman," she said darkly, then laughed. "A typical case of don't do as I do, et cetera."

Dan watched and heard her laugh and was enchanted. She looked even younger than usual, and carefree. And he realized how rare it was that she really laughed and that, in spite of her generally youthful appearance and seemingly boundless energy, an air of worry and care overshadowed her around the edges. He found himself wishing he could ase her burdens, assume them for his own. Make her life happy, secure...

Suddenly aware of Dan's intent scrutiny, Lisa lifted questioning eyes and felt a scorching blush stain her cheeks at the unexpected and unguarded expression she caught on his face. An expression much like the one she had glimpsed just before he had kissed her that night at his apartment.

Disconcerted by his look, as well as by her body's response to it, she looked down into her coffee cup again. She picked up a spoon and noisily stirred the black liquid.

"Where would we be staying?" she asked, mostly for the sake of something to say, but also because it had just occurred to her that not only she, but Dan Morgan, too, might be tempted by things other than business on this trip.

Dan took a deep breath and chided himself for making her feel ill at ease. Would he never learn to guard his expressions, to tread carefully around this contradictory creature? Would he never remember that her show of nonchalance and savvy disguised a remarkably untouched and sensitive soul? And that, all things considered, only a professional relationship between them could be acceptable?

"We'll both be in a hotel on Saturday, the day we arrive," he said, "but on Sunday we move you into a small furnished place of your own. Modest, as befits your means as a down-and-out warehouseperson. But clean," he hastened to add. He paused, his expression serious. "This is a business trip, Lisa. Period. Do you understand what I'm saying?"

She looked up with a lopsided smile. "Sure. I understand. And thank you."

She saw relief lighten his troubled features and told herself that was what she felt, too.

Alaska, Lisa thought. *Somewhere underneath all this gray stuff lies America's last frontier.*

"On a clear day the view of Anchorage is spectacular," Dan said as they prepared to land. "Sparkling blue waters, majestic mountains..."

"You just had to say that, didn't you?" Lisa groused, sourly watching the thick clouds accompany the aircraft's descent right down to the ground. When at last the gray curtain parted, the dreary, rain-soaked countryside did nothing to cheer her.

"Look at this, we might as well be back in Seattle," she complained. "At the very least I expected to see snow. After all, this is late September in the rugged North."

"Not all that rugged, you'll find, nor all that north, relatively speaking." Dan was amused by Lisa's disgruntled expression. She looked like a kid who had just discovered the circus tiger had no teeth.

"On the first fine day we'll go sight-seeing," he promised, ushering her through the jetway into the terminal.

"No, we won't. We'll be at work."

"Right. On the first fine day *off*, then."

That made her brighten, which in turn pleased Dan. They collected their luggage and he rented a modest car. Modest because, as the lowly security agent Jeff Myers, anything larger would have been out of place.

Arriving at the Prospector's Inn, Lisa gasped at the luxury of their accommodations and questioned the wisdom of staying at such a prestigious hotel.

Dan waved her objections aside. "I have no intention of socializing with my fellow workers, and I do intend to be comfortable. It's bad enough to be courting a permanent cramp in the legs from this car."

He grinned at her. "And you, young lady, might as well enjoy a few luxuries the only night you get to stay in a hotel. It's on the expense account—and I have an in with the boss, remember?"

"Ah, yes."

They registered separately, Lisa reading every line of the card with care before she filled it in. This was the first time she had ever done this, but not for the world did she want Dan to know that.

They had adjacent rooms on the tenth floor, but there was no connecting door to threaten Lisa's peace of mind. Perversely, instead of offering reassurance, this vaguely annoyed and disappointed her. It was one thing to be morally prepared to resist Dan Morgan's advances, but quite another to find that he really had not intended to make any.

Her suitcase was full of her usual clothes—John and Dan had assured her they'd be prefect for this assignment—but she had brought her navy blue suit and intended to wear it that night. There was plenty of time for a shower before going to dinner at six. Lisa's stomach growled as if on cue, oblivious to the fact that they had gained an hour and it was not yet time to eat in Anchorage, Alaska.

She had just finished blow-drying her hair when someone knocked.

It was Dan, looking disturbingly fresh and crisp in blue blazer and gray slacks. He was holding up a Morgan's garment bag.

"I was wondering if I could ask you a favor," he said with a smile, his eyes traveling warmly over every shining inch of her scrubbed face.

Lisa looked from Dan to the garment bag and back to Dan. "What?" she asked suspiciously.

"Wear this dress to dinner tonight."

Lisa gasped. The nerve of him. Hadn't she made it clear that she wanted none of his charity?

"I will not," she stated emphatically, and made to slam the door in his face.

Dan stopped her by firmly pressing his palm against the wooden panel. "Wait," he said with a twinkle in his eye that seemed to warn of impending mischief, "You don't understand. You see, I'm conducting a fashion survey and I've distributed the exact same dress to every woman on this floor. In varying sizes, of course. Now, by the merest coincidence I just happen to have this one left.''

He looked down at her shapeless robe while Lisa fought a losing battle against the smile that was trying to emerge.

''In that robe it's hard to tell, of course,'' Dan continued thoughtfully, ''but I'm pretty sure it's your size. Anyway, after you put it on, here's what happens: At precisely six o'clock all you ladies will line up in the hall, and a completely impartial panel of judges will determine which one of you looks the best in this dress. The winner gets to keep the thing. Come on, what do you say?''

By this time Lisa was shaking her head and laughing helplessly. How could she resist such an imaginative spiel without being utterly boorish? She reached to take the dress from him.

''Why do I get the feeling that, in spite of the Morgan's bag, I've seen this dress before?'' she asked pointedly.

Dan grinned and shrugged. ''Beats me.''

''Yes, well, since all the other ladies were gracious enough to participate, it wouldn't be very nice of me to refuse, would it?''

''No, it wouldn't,'' Dan said stoutly, his eyes gleaming. ''Thank you, Miss Hanrahan. You're a real sport.''

Lisa closed the door.

When she opened it again, sharply at six, she was glad she had agreed to wear the dress. The look of undisguised male appreciation on Dan's face bathed her in a glow of pleasure. ''Well?'' she asked with uncharacteristic coyness, suddenly wanting to hear the words, too.

''Wow,'' Dan breathed, stepping back to take in every colorful silk-clad inch of her. ''It's no contest. You're definitely the winner, Miss Hanrahan.'' He turned toward the row of imaginary women out in the hall. ''Strip, ladies. The contest is over.''

Lisa laughed. "You're the impartial panel of judges, I presume?"

"How'd you guess?"

"Oh, call it a hunch. Woman's intuition."

Dan joined her laughter, and that set the tone for the rest of the evening.

They enjoyed a wonderful meal of prime rib in a favorite restaurant of Dan's, surrounded by memorabilia of the city's gold rush and pioneering days. Their lighthearted banter didn't let up until they were once again in front of Lisa's door, this time to part for the night.

Dan took the key out of her unresisting fingers and unlocked the door, pushing it slightly ajar.

Suddenly tongue-tied and short of breath, Lisa clutched her tiny purse and prepared to enter with a choked, "Good night."

Dan placed a staying hand on her arm.

Slowly Lisa turned to face him, to look up into his eyes. They were glowing now with the special light that could so easily spark a heated response in her own. Already swarms of butterflies seemed to have taken wing in her stomach.

"You said strictly business," she felt compelled to remind him, but did not resist when Dan lifted her arms and placed them around his neck.

"Just a good-night kiss for the judge," he murmured, intently watching the tip of Lisa's tongue as it moistened her parted lips. "That's my part of the prize."

"You didn't say anything about that before," Lisa whispered shakily, tempted—oh, so tempted—to just once more give in to her clamoring senses. Just to feel. Just to see if it was really as magical as she remembered.

"Would you have taken the dress if I had?"

"No," she breathed even as she rose onto her toes and pressed her body to his.

Chapter Six

Lisa's fingers tentatively stroked the fine hairs at Dan's nape, tangled briefly in the thicker strands above, then slid down to frame his face. Gently she stroked the faintly abrasive planes and angles, tracing their outline down to his chin until her thumbs came to rest at the corners of his mouth. She pressed against them lightly, experimentally, and with a low growl Dan's lips claimed hers.

His hands slipped inside her unbuttoned coat, there to stroke and shape the softness of her silk-clad curves as he kissed her. Softly at first. His lips merely brushed and tantalized, coaxed and instructed. And then, unable not to, he went deeper. His tongue teased hers, catching and releasing, all the while tasting of the sweetness he had known would be there for him.

Lisa moaned weakly and clung to Dan as once she had clung to the trunk of that tall maple she had climbed at her father's parsonage. The frightening yet exhilarating things

Dan's kiss was making her feel were not unlike those she had felt then.

The quaking limbs, the pervading sensation of weakness, the fear of tumbling down, down, down into some nameless and unknown peril. Yet, she was no longer frightened by those sensations, merely stunned. And craving more.

She fit herself closer to him, widened the shape of her lips, pursued and captured his clever tongue with her own, caressed it as he was showing her to do. She felt heavy with languor, yet light-headed, too. She shivered, yet had never felt this hot.

"Lisa." Thoroughly shaken by her eager response, Dan's mouth slanted across hers with suddenly ravenous need.

A whimper escaped Lisa's throat and was swallowed by his kiss. Though the tiny sound had not been one of protest, Dan lightened the kiss and slowly drew back. Little by little, he allowed her feet to touch the floor again, then pressed one last lingering kiss on her mouth before lifting his head. His hands once more smoothed across her hips, then reached up to unclasp her fingers from behind his neck.

Lisa's lids fluttered, then reluctantly lifted. Momentarily disoriented, her eyes not quite able to focus, she gazed up at Dan. He was smiling tenderly, his thumbs stroking the backs of her hands as he held them tightly between their heated bodies.

He leaned down once more and dropped a kiss onto the tip of her nose.

"Good night," he whispered and, with one last squeeze, released her hands.

As if in a trance, Lisa watched him walk the few steps to his door and unlock it. She half raised her hand in a dreamy gesture of farewell as, with a jaunty wink in her direction, he stepped inside. She let the hand drop and released a shaky breath. An odd sense of unappeased hunger gnawed at the pit of her stomach, a longing for more. A regret for promises not fulfilled.

Slowly, at once bemused and enlivened by the curious mixture of her emotions, Lisa, too, entered her room.

She awoke to brilliant sunshine filtering through the slats of the venetian blind, creating a striped pattern alive with tiny particles of dust. Yawning hugely, her arms aloft in a delicious stretch, Lisa was happy to find that last evening's sense of exhilaration had survived the restless, dream-filled night.

In the face of this glorious morning she was ready to accept the fact of her attraction to Daniel Morgan. She was ready to admit to the joy his kiss had brought. It was time, she decided, *past* time, for her to enjoy a taste of romance. Other women her age, Marcia for one, seemed constantly to be indulging in it with no ill effects. The trick seemed to be to keep it in perspective, to keep it light.

In her case, since Dan was her employer, that meant not letting what had transpired interfere with her work. Nor to allow a couple of kisses to seduce her into thinking that should lead to further kisses—and more. She didn't want more. When this weekend was over, this short detour from her chosen path would end, too.

Today, though, was still special. It was a day off from work, from reality. The sun was shining. All the ingredients were there for the day of sight-seeing Dan had promised.

Full of anticipation, Lisa jumped out of bed. She dashed into the bathroom and broke into song beneath the shower's stinging spray. Wrapped in a towel, she was just rushing back into her room to dress when the phone rang.

"Hello!" Her expression matched the sun's brightness when Dan identified himself on the other end.

"You sound good and chirpy this morning," he said, sounding pretty chipper himself. "It's your moving day, so how about breakfast in half an hour?"

"Sounds good."

They met in the hall outside their rooms and stood still for a moment to contemplate each other's expressions as if searching for regrets. Finding none, they exchanged pleased grins and joined an elderly couple for the elevator ride down to the lobby.

The restaurant was sparsely peopled at this relatively early hour, and they were immediately seated. Conversation between them was punctuated by odd moments of self-consciousness and largely confined to comments on the huge breakfast of bacon-cheese-and-mushroom-laden omelets they devoured along with mounds of fluffy homemade biscuits.

"Enjoy it while you can," Dan urged Lisa when she began to groan halfway through the mountain of food in front of her. "Since it's your last meal served in style on the expense account. After this, you'll be your own cook for a while."

"Bite your tongue." Lisa dabbed at her mouth with the napkin. "Nobody, least of all I, should be reduced to eating *my* cooking."

"All the more reason to dig in now. One more bite and I'll drive you to your new home. Afterward, since the sun is out and if you're good, we'll play tourist."

"If I'm good?"

Dan's grin widened as indignation at his choice of words predictably raised Lisa's voice an octave.

Lisa's apartment turned out to be one unit in a long row of single-story wooden cabins that constituted the Northern Lights Motel. Once white, now peeling, the place was no castle but, in spite of those signs of neglect, clusters of late-blooming mums along its facade lent color and cheer to the drabness.

The front door of Unit D, Lisa's home, opened into a combination living room-kitchen-dinette, with a small bedroom and bath beyond. Though the furnishings were recycled fifties horrors in faded oranges and browns, the rooms were clean, the bed only slightly lumpy and the bathroom enamel chipped but gleaming.

Lisa was content, having lived in worse places, but Daniel was less than enchanted. He hated the thought of this bright and vibrant young woman stuck in this dreary hole in the wall night after night while he languished in luxury at the Prospector's Inn.

"I can't believe this is the best Davidson could do, in spite of the shortage of temporary housing here," he grumbled, bouncing on the sofa to test its springs. He decided it had none.

"Who's Davidson?"

Lisa had finished her cursory inspection of the kitchen cabinets and appliances and joined him on the couch. "Well, this is nice and firm," she said, bouncing, too.

"Yeah." Dan's look was wry. "Like a church pew."

"Listen, I've sat in plenty of those in my time, and believe me, this is softer." Lisa bounced again and grimaced. "Not much, though. Who's Davidson?"

"The Anchorage store manager. And remember the name." Dan cautiously tried leaning against the sofa's back. "He's the only person here who knows our true identities and purpose. If you get in trouble and can't get ahold of me, you call him, understood?"

"Aye-aye, sir."

"Brat." Dan eyed her sternly and felt an immediate and unsettling tightening of throat and loins at the beguiling picture she made with mischief glowing in her eyes. He jumped up from the couch.

"Come on, you," he said, a trifle gruffly, "let's go take a look at our temporary hometown."

Though it was noon, the city streets were quiet on this lovely Sunday. The day was as glorious as the bright streaks through the slats of Lisa's hotel room window blinds had promised—brilliantly clear, but with a hint of crispness to remind them that winter was just one good freeze away. Snowcapped mountains scalloped the horizon like a jagged saw's teeth beneath an azure sky.

Lisa was all eyes, looking this way and that, frequently craning her neck for a second look.

"Isn't this neat?" She clearly expected no answer and Dan gave none. He enjoyed her enthusiasm, slanting many an indulgent glance in her direction. The flush of her cheek, the sparkle of those dark, liquid eyes, the hands primly clasped in her lap. What a bundle of contradictions Lisa Hanrahan was. What a confounding and intriguing combination of zany self-assuredness, unspoilt innocence and fierce pride.

Without even trying, she touched something inside of him that no one, man or woman, ever had. She moved him in a myriad of ways and elicited responses that ran the gamut from fury to laughter to tenderness.

The only feeling she had never roused in him was boredom, he thought with a wry inward smile. And he doubted she ever would, even if they were to share a lifetime.

A frown lowered Dan's brow and replaced his smile. How had lifetimes gotten into his aimless contemplations? And how quickly could that ridiculous notion be gotten rid of?

Vexed with himself, he swung his gaze back to the road just in time to notice that his car, like his thoughts, had drifted where it should not and was perilously close to rubbing fenders with a stately Mercedes-Benz.

With a strained smile of apology to its glaring driver, Dan hastened to swerve back into his own lane.

Lisa, question marks in her eyes, reached out and briefly laid the back of her hand against his cheek.

"Are you all right?" She leaned close to peer worriedly into his face. "Your cheek feels warm, and you're looking a little flushed. Did something at breakfast not agree with you?"

Dan felt her touch like a brand and stifled a groan. Sternly he ordered himself to get his act together.

"I'm fine," he assured her after clearing his throat, then, anxious to reclaim the shield of their earlier banter, added, "Just wanted to wake you up."

"Wake me up?" Lisa took immediate and predictable umbrage. "I'll have you know that I wasn't the one sleeping, you were. And in the process you almost sideswiped that fancy car, which would've cost you a month's salary in repairs."

"That much?"

"At least. Remember, you're only a lowly security agent now, not the wealthy heir of a string of department stores."

"You don't like wealthy heirs?" Dan meant to tease, but found himself all but holding his breath as he waited for Lisa's reply.

It came in the form of a half snort, half laugh, followed by an evasion. "Did I say that?"

"Your tone inferred it."

"Then I'm sorry."

"You are? Why, for Pete's sake?"

"Well, you're nice enough to take me out, the last thing I want to do is spoil this day—"

"Spoil this day?" Dan stared at her, astounded. "How?"

"By fighting with you—"

"Fighting? About what?"

"If you didn't keep interrupting me, you'd know already."

Dan's gaze on her narrowed. "So tell me."

"About . . . you know, people. Money . . ."

"Aah!" Dan's sigh was explosive, his nod one of exasperated agreement. "That. You're right, this is not the day for it."

They drove in silence for a while, both staring straight ahead.

"Mr. Morgan—"

"Myers," Dan interjected. "Jeff Myers, remember?" His smile told her their previous exchange was forgotten.

Lisa's smile told Dan how much she appreciated that. "Thank you," she said.

"You're enjoying the tour so far?"

"Oh, yes." With a sigh of relief Lisa turned to look out the window again. "It's hard to take it all in. This is my first time out of Washington State, you know."

"No kidding?" Dan meant no offense with this dry rejoinder, and Lisa took none. She sent him an arched look, though.

"I suppose you've been all over the world and to you this is old hat?" she said.

"Pretty much, in answer to the first part of your question. No, to the second." Dan couldn't help the warm glance he sent her. "Thanks to you, I'm enjoying this outing more than the safari I went on in Africa."

"Safari?" Their gazes briefly collided. Lisa's was full of outrage again. "As in hunting animals?"

"As in taking pictures. A photo safari."

"Oh." Lisa felt foolish. "Well, thank God for that," she mumbled. She ignored Dan's chuckle and stared out the window again.

"Where are we going?"

Dan had been driving without a clear destination in mind and had to take a moment to get his bearings. They were on Highway 1 and had all but left the city and its tracts of houses and construction sites behind.

"We're heading toward Turnagain Arm," he said, adding the rest of their itinerary as it occurred to him. "We'll follow it all the way to Portage Glacier and up to Mount Alyeska. How's that grab you?"

"Turnagain Arm, huh? Neat name. Any ideas how it came about?"

Dan shook his head. "'Fraid not. I suspect it has to do with the fact that the Arm ends at Portage, and that the only way to get back to town is to turn around again. In any case, it's a spectacular drive, in part along either water or mud—depending on the tide. Wait and see, you'll be impressed."

Lisa was. Everywhere she looked, the scenery was breathtaking. The icebergs at Portage Glacier, partially melted into shapes of abstract beauty, sparkled in the sun like blue sapphires.

Mount Alyeska rose majestically, its base already lightly dusted with the first snows of winter. They lunched on beer and German wurst with sauerkraut in a small chalet near the ski lifts. Afterward they hiked among the tall pines, inhaling deeply of their invigorating scent.

On the drive back toward the city, Dan suddenly pulled off the road and jumped out of the car. He ran to open Lisa's door and, ignoring her startled exclamation, dragged her out. Draping an arm over her shoulders, he leaned his head close.

"Look," he whispered, pointing up toward some craggy cliffs. "Mountain goats."

Their cheeks touched and tingled as if from sparks of static electricity. Lisa's breath trembled as her eyes followed Dan's pointing finger.

She gasped with delight when she spotted the animals, so splendid in their shaggy white coats, proudly curved horns and pointed beards. They were placidly grazing on tufts of shrubbery growing out of cracks in a rocky mountainside that seemed too steep to grant them a foothold.

"Look at them, way up there," she exclaimed in an awed whisper, as if to speak in a normal voice might startle them and cause them to slip, fall. She turned to Dan with shining eyes. "They're beautiful."

And so are you, Dan thought. So are you. Her mouth was so near, and in her excitement, so temptingly parted. More than anything on earth, Dan wanted to kiss it. But he didn't. In light of the startling and unexpected emotions Lisa aroused in him, Dan had come to realize that it was imperative he understand both them and his intentions before getting involved any more deeply than he already was.

And so he returned her incandescent smile with one of considerably less wattage and moved away a little before once more admiring those agile creatures on the barren rocks above.

They drove back to the city without talking much, each content in thought.

Lisa was reliving every moment of this special day and marveled at the ease she felt in Dan Morgan's company. It was easy to forget their respective roles of employer and employee when they were like this—just a man and a woman enjoying each other. She had never experienced anything like it before with a man. John and Marc didn't count, they were like brothers to her—comfortable, unexciting.

Dan was different, the feelings he inspired were different. They were feelings no one else had ever been able to arouse in her—not that she had given anyone else a chance. Perhaps she should have. Perhaps she owed it to herself to find out if other men could. Somehow the idea held little appeal.

They made a brief stop at a supermarket.

"Just coffee, dry cereal, milk, juice and fruit, that's all I need," Lisa declared. "Breakfast is the only meal I intend to eat in."

On the way to her apartment, they ate a light dinner at a nearby fast-food place, then, all too soon as far as Lisa was concerned, it was time to part.

Dan too hated to see the day end. The thought of returning to his hotel room alone was depressing, the urge to linger, to kiss Lisa's lips, overwhelming. Aware that the first was inevitable and the second unthinkable under the circumstances, Dan sought refuge in his employer persona.

His tone was brisk as he bid her good-night and added, "Since you don't know how to drive, I'll be picking you up and dropping you off every day. Other than that, however, I think it would be best if we associated as little as possible. You can give me your daily progress reports in the car. Is that agreeable?"

Lisa nodded, very much aware that she had just been neatly and firmly put back in her place.

"That's perfectly agreeable," she said, her tone stiff with injured pride. She wasted no time getting out of the car. Her slam of the door drowned out Dan's heartfelt, self-directed curse, and she didn't turn back to see the look of chagrin that clouded his handsome face.

Lisa's warehouse position as receiving clerk was, to her, a boring battle with paperwork in a place as big as a barn but not nearly as homey. Rows upon rows of towering shelves loaded with boxes, crates and cartons of all manner of merchandise formed avenues where forklifts were a constant menace to the unwary person on foot.

It was Lisa's job, with the help of a computer, to know the general location of every item of inventory as, from her desk right inside the entrance of the building, she directed the delivery and removal of merchandise. She checked in bills of lading, checked out purchase orders, always comparing the items inside any given crate or carton against the numbers on the papers. The work was intellectually undemanding and allowed her mind too much freedom to drift where she'd rather it didn't.

To Dan, of course. Both she and he were strenuously polite and correct in the limited conversations they shared on the short rides to and from work. Their easy friendship of the previous weekend might never have been; their brush with passion might never have occurred.

Which, so she told herself, was as it should be, of course.

They talked of work, period. Not that she had much to report to him during that first week, though by the end of it, suspicions had begun to form in her mind. Security in the warehouse facility seemed to her, token, at best. There were ample opportunities for theft, and she told him as much.

That weekend, Dan claimed to be scheduled for work. On her part, Lisa said her studies, the laundry and things like that would keep her very busy anyway. On Monday, both were full of feigned enthusiasm about the kind of weekend they'd had. And each resented hearing it from the other.

Toward the end of the second week, Lisa's suspicions had firmed. Her list of suspects had been reduced to one man. Jack Wilson. There had been two incidents where a box he had unloaded was short an item of merchandise.

On the one occasion, Lisa had been on lunch break. The warehouseman who spelled her then, had made a notation that they were short one record turntable. Just a few days earlier, during her weekend off, it had been a fur-lined man's jacket. Wilson had been involved then, too. Coincidence? Lisa didn't think so.

She kept her eye on the man for the next couple of days and learned that he not only unloaded trucks but also hauled empty boxes and cartons out to the Dumpster behind the warehouse. A light clicked on in her head.

Hadn't she heard somewhere of a scam whereby supposedly missing items of merchandise had actually been put into the trash and later retrieved? Hmm!

She decided some afterhours detecting was in order.

Not wanting to divulge her theories before they were fact, Lisa phoned over to security to tell Dan she wouldn't need a ride home that evening. He was out on a break, so she left a message.

Two hours later he sauntered in. Lisa's heart did a quick somersault that was not entirely due to the thrill of seeing him. A bit of apprehension contributed, as well. He would not like it if he knew the real reason she wouldn't be needing a ride that night.

"You didn't tell me you had plans for the evening," he said, eyeing her intently across the littered expanse of her desk.

Lisa shrugged, not comfortable in the role she had set for herself. *Lying lips are an abomination to the Lord* . . . How often her father had quoted that. Her eyes strayed from Dan's too-close regard.

"Something came up." Which wasn't a lie, was it?

"Such as?" Dan's famous frown now shadowed his piercing gaze. He braced himself on his knuckles and leaned his face close. "You don't know anybody in this town. What're you up to?"

"Up to?" A mixture of guilt and resentment brought Lisa to her feet. "I'd say that was none of your business, Mr. Mo—Myers. I'm of age and I'll do as I please."

"You're in Anchorage under *my* supervision, and you'll do as *I* please."

"On the job. Not on my own time."

They glowered at each other. Neither spoke, neither wanted to back off. The silence between them fairly crackled with hostile vibrations.

Dan knew she was right, her own time was her business. But—dammit, she was a stranger in this town. Besides which, a feeling in his gut told him she was up to something. He tried to decipher the odd mixture of emotions flitting across her expressive face but couldn't get beyond defiance and stubbornness.

"Fine." He barked the word like a curse. "Great." He backed away, palms up. "Have it your way."

Lisa pressed her lips together to keep from saying, "I'll explain later. Don't be angry." And watched with burning eyes as he wrenched open the door and stalked out of the warehouse.

The scene left her depressed and not nearly as eager as she had been to pursue her suspicions. This in turn made her mad at herself. Since when did she worry about someone else's opinion of her when her goals were at stake? She wouldn't be where she was today if she'd heeded anything but her own conscience all these years.

Trouble was, it was her conscience that bothered her. They had, after all, agreed to work together on this. Lisa frowned, chewed her lip, stewed. And finally convinced herself that what she was doing was right. She had only a hunch; it might well come to nothing. Why put another person at risk, especially one as unfamiliar with security and self-defense as Daniel Morgan?

She worked till the warehouse closed at nine and took her time leaving the premises. Outside she headed around the building for the street with purposeful strides, trying to look as though she were walking toward a real destination and not just pretending.

It was a dark, raw, drizzly sort of night, and she suspected that the fine rain might easily turn to snow a few hours and a few more downward-plunging degrees later. Her breath came out in puffs of steam as she moved toward the lighted street, shoulders hunched and hands buried deep inside her pockets.

When it seemed all her fellow employees had either driven off or disappeared on foot, Lisa turned back the way she had come. With one last, cautious look around, she

crouched down near the large Dumpster by a loading ramp.
And settled down to wait.

To keep from noticing the chills that soon began to creep
up her legs and back, she concentrated on warm, pleasant
thoughts. Dan Morgan's face, the sudden smiles that
changed it so... But then the smiles were gone and he was
frowning at her, glaring his disapproval. Oh, damn.

A bump against the metal followed by a scraping sort of
sound from the other side of the Dumpster abruptly yanked
Lisa from the half-hypnotized state she had inadvertently
allowed herself to slip into.

The thief! He was there. And by the sound of it, climb-
ing into the trash container.

Adrenaline rushed into every limb. It urged Lisa to leap
up and confront the thief. She forced herself to be calm, to
think, not just react.

Very carefully, head down, shoulders hunched, knees bent
in a low crouch, she shuffled toward the sound. At the corner of the container she risked a quick peek around it. A bit
of leg and a booted foot were just disappearing over the top
into the Dumpster.

Lisa pulled back, pressed herself against the cold metal
side of it. The thump of the person landing was accompanied by a low curse and the sound of scrunching card-
board, and reverberated through her taut body.

She jerked away, straightened, retreated a few steps. Her
mind was frantically scrambling for a battle plan, an idea
how best to proceed—

Still in retreat, her back bumped into something firm. She
froze, gasped, barely managed to swallow the shriek that
leaped into her throat.

Good grief! she thought, electrified. *An accomplice!*

Everything that followed was pure reflex.

Spinning, she grabbed a handful of sleeve in both hands,
bent, twisted her wrists and neatly tossed her would-be-

assailant overhand and to the ground. Without pausing, she dove full-length onto his prone form and stuck two pointed fingers into his ribs.

"Don't move unless you like to bleed," she hissed, punctuating each word with a stab of the fingers and praying they felt like the tip of a knife.

The man grunted. He made to shake her off. Lisa jerked up her knee, fully intending to damage a very vulnerable area of the man's anatomy.

"No!" As though he had sensed her intent, the man twisted his torso and had Lisa pinned beneath him before she could react. A large hand was clamped over her mouth. His face was just inches from hers.

"Not a sound," he growled, "not a move, you hear me?"

White-faced with shock, Lisa could do no more than blink her assent—and shiver beneath the blast of icy fury from Dan Morgan's eyes.

Chapter Seven

You little fool," Dan raged. His hands still clamped over Lisa's mouth, his body rigid on top of hers, he looked ready to commit murder. "Why didn't you tell me you'd—"

Sounds of scrambling and scraping and the thud of feet hitting the ground abruptly cut short the rest of his invective. He levered himself off her and was up on his feet in one swift movement that was testimony to his fine physical condition.

At any other time, Lisa might have been impressed, but right then she was intent only on catching her breath and getting herself up off the ground to join the chase after their fleeing suspect. Pushing everything, especially the stab of trepidation she felt when contemplating Dan's wrath, to the back of her mind, she concentrated on the dark shapes running ahead of her.

Dan was gaining on the suspect, Lisa noted with relief. Maybe all was not lost. Her feet pounded the wet pavement of the parking lot. Her breath came in panting gasps. But she was not able to close the gap between herself and the men. The unforeseen tussle with Dan had knocked the wind out of her, and she couldn't quite recapture it.

The men were beneath one of the tall parking lot lights when Dan lunged for the suspect's legs in a stylish tackle that would have made any football coach proud.

Forcing her heaving lungs to draw breath and her feet to move more swiftly, Lisa gave a silent cheer as she watched them crash to the ground.

The suspect immediately scrambled to regain his feet, but Dan's arms effectively manacled the guy's knees. He fell again. Dan squirmed, shimmying upward for a better grip.

Lisa pushed herself to even greater speed, closing in on them, ready to do her part. She winced when the suspect's foot connected smartly with the side of Dan's head and shared the pain Dan's guttural bellow told her he felt.

Outrage translated itself into adrenaline, and she fairly flew across the blacktop in pursuit of the once-again fleeing suspect. Seconds later momentum and her body weight combined to form a missile that slammed into the man's back. He toppled like a felled tree.

Lisa was sprawled, panting, on top of him but immediately scrambled to straddle his inert form. The man didn't stir.

Cautiously, hoping but not sure that the fall had knocked him out, she leaned over to peer into his face. So, she thought, pursing lips in grim satisfaction. Her suspicions were confirmed. It was Wilson, all right.

Lisa was still congratulating herself when, without warning, Wilson moved. In the blink of an eye she was tossed off the man's back and onto her own.

Bloodied teeth in a snarling mouth and a raised fist were all she saw before she squeezed her eyes tightly shut in anticipation of the crushing blow she knew was coming. Braced for the exploding agony, it took a moment for her to register the sudden loss of pressure against her rib cage and the sound of a fist thudding into flesh.

Her eyes popped open. Dan was holding her assailant by the scruff of his jacket with one hand, while his other was the fist now driving into the man's midsection. Wilson grunted and doubled over.

Dan, his face filthy and distorted into a savage mask, hauled back for another punishing blow.

"No!" Lisa cried, lunging to her feet and catching his arm with both hands. "Dan! Stop! Please! It's over."

For a moment it seemed he hadn't heard her, even tried to shake her off. She tightened her grip. Their eyes clashed. Hers pleaded. His, bloodshot and glazed, seemed to deny. Then he shook his head as if to clear water out of his ears, his eyes regained focus, and the arm she was clutching relaxed and lowered.

"He was going to hit you," he said, his voice little more than a hoarse growl deep in the back of his throat.

"I know."

Their eyes did a rapid search of each other's faces, assuring themselves the other was all right. A nasty bruise was beginning to discolor the side of Dan's face, but there was no blood.

With an audible quiver, Lisa let go the breath she'd been holding. Oh, God, she thought, what if he'd been seriously hurt....

Dan was equally shaken by the might-have-beens. He let go of the suspect and, oblivious to the fact that the man sagged to the ground like a Slinky toy collapsing onto itself, hauled Lisa against his chest and held her there. "Are you all right?"

"Yes." Lisa's face was pressed into Dan's chest. Dizzy with relief and reaction, she absorbed the rapid tattoo of his heart and was warmed by the heat of him through his damp sweatshirt. "I'm fine."

She was more than fine, she thought dimly, reveling in the moment of respite that allowed her to enjoy the feel and smell of him.

A moment was all she had, for suddenly Dan's frantically stroking hands were gentle no more. They closed around her upper arms like clamps of iron and jerked her away from his body.

Startled, Lisa glanced up sharply. Dan's eyes were ablaze.

"I could kill you for this fool stunt," he snarled, "and still may. Just as soon as we get this joker booked."

Dan hadn't made good his threat, of course, though as he stood beneath the hot shower spray pelting his aching body, the thought of strangling Lisa's independent little neck was still decidedly tempting. What he *had* done, after dispensing with the preliminary process of getting their thief into police custody, was to stuff her into the car, deposit her at her place and, with dire warnings of the consequences should she set one foot outside the door, had dragged himself to his hotel. They would talk in the morning, when he hoped to be calmer.

Morning had come but not the calm. After a restless night filled with nightmare visions of Lisa battered and bloodied at his feet, Dan's temper was on a short fuse. It ignited just as soon as she answered his knock.

"Don't you know better than to open the door to anyone without asking who it is?"

Lisa's eyes widened, then narrowed. "Good morning to you, too," she murmured, standing aside as he charged past her into the room.

He spun and glared at her. "Why didn't you tell me about this Wilson character as soon as you suspected him? Why did you lie to me yesterday afternoon?"

Lisa took her time closing the door before turning to face him. She had spent the night rehashing every minute of every ghastly scene and realized she had been foolhardy in thinking she could handle things alone. This morning she'd been ready to tell Dan so, to explain her reasoning, to even— God help her—apologize. But his tone, his attitude of righteous male wrath, forestalled that now.

She folded her arms tightly across her chest, girding for battle. She raised her chin.

"I did not lie to you," she said as coolly as she was able in the face of Dan's white-hot glare. "I simply didn't think I should tell you anything because all I *had* were suspicions. Last night I wanted—"

"You wanted to be a hero," Dan snarled. "God forbid you should ask for help."

"I didn't think I needed help," Lisa said hotly. "All I was going to do was watch to see what, if anything, went on with that Dumpster at night. Then *you* came along, scaring me half out of my wits and bungling—"

"Bungling? *Bungling?* It wasn't me who bungled, Miss Hanrahan. I gave you strict orders to report *everything* you saw to me. Every evening. Not just when it suited you, and not just an edited version of what was really going on. Last night you deliberately lied to me."

"I said I had other plans and wouldn't need a ride," Lisa shot back. Being cool no longer mattered, making him see that she didn't lie, did. "That's not lying. It isn't. I never lie."

"You lied last night," Dan said flatly. He took a deep breath and raked a shaky hand through his hair as he abruptly turned and traversed the room. At the far end, he faced her again.

"We are on this case together, Lisa," he said, seeming immeasurably weary as he massaged the back of his neck and stared at her. "You had no right to proceed on your own, no right to place yourself in that kind of danger. But not only that, you nearly ruined our chances of catching this guy. You blew your cover, and if he'd gotten away that would've been the end of our case, period."

"But he didn't get away," Lisa argued. "We got him and—"

"*We* got him, yes." Dan cut off her protestations with renewed anger and impatience. "The point is, *you* wouldn't have. Not alone."

"I never intended to," Lisa cried. "All I was going to do was observe."

"Without being observed back, of course," Dan ground out sarcastically. Three long strides brought him within inches of her. "What if he'd seen you? What if there'd been two of them? Three? What if they'd been armed? What if—"

"All right. All *right*." Lisa covered her ears and backed up a step. She glared at him. Though inwardly she cringed with the knowledge that Dan was right, she was in no mood to grant him that aloud. "So what're you planning to do now, fire me?"

"The thought had crossed my mind, yes."

"Well, in that case let me save you the trouble." Lisa's temper was in charge now, not her brain. "I quit."

"Terrific. Thank you."

"You're welcome. And listen to this. I've been planning to quit all along. I was only waiting to complete my M.B.A."

"I see."

"And I only fought your plan of transferring me to another department so I could prove I'm as good a security agent as anyone. I—"

Suddenly feeling quite sick about the way she was acting, Lisa broke off. Her throat worked to swallow the brick stuck sideways in it. It wouldn't budge. She stared at Dan in helpless misery.

He stared back for interminable moments of silence. His face was devoid of expression, his eyes cold. "Well," he said at length, his tone clipped and businesslike. "That seems to be that. Your check, Miss Hanrahan, will be in the mail."

He shouldered past her and stalked to the door. He wrenched it open.

"I . . . I'll work until a replacement's been hired," Lisa offered hesitantly.

Dan stood still. Staring straight ahead, he said, "Thank you, but that won't be necessary."

Lisa briefly considered telling him she needed the money, but both conscience and pride forbade it. She had heaped this mess on her plate unaided, it was only right she should have to swallow it the same way.

Dan slowly turned. He scanned her face, hesitated, then said, "Though the events of last night might tend to dispute it, you did prove to be a far better security agent than I ever expected. I've learned a lot during our brief association, and I thank you for that."

"Dan, I . . ." Lisa faltered, miserable that after all the other battles they'd fought in order to come to terms with each other, things should end this way. "I'm sorry," she offered softly. "I wish—"

"Yes." Dan nodded once, his face grim. "So do I."

Lisa's solitary flight back to Seattle two days later was nothing like the exciting, anticipation-filled trip in the opposite direction had been. She slept through most of it in a futile effort to escape her relentlessly taunting thoughts. Fool, they called her, over and over. Fool, fool, fool . . .

John Turner was waiting for her at Seattle-Tacoma airport. His expression was unreadable. Lisa braced herself for a scathing dressing-down, but it never came.

"Good flight?" John inquired, fallng into step beside her.

"It was fine."

"You nabbed the warehouse thief. Congratulations."

"Th-thanks." She glanced at him sideways. "Have you talked with Dan Morgan lately?"

"Yup. He's the one who told me to meet your flight."

"Oh. I thought it was the twins."

"Nope. It was Morgan."

John let her precede him onto the escalator, and they rode down to baggage claim without speaking.

"Heard you quit," he said when they'd reached the bottom.

"Yes."

"A bit premature, wasn't it?"

"It seemed like the thing to do at the time."

"Care to tell me about it?"

"Didn't Da—Mr. Morgan?"

"No. He only said you wouldn't be back, but to pay you till the end of October. Nice guy—"

"What?" Lisa stopped in her tracks, and a man laden with luggage crashed into her back. She stumbled forward. The man dropped his bags and cursed. John caught and steadied Lisa. She was oblivious to it all, squealing, "He *what*?"

"I have never in all my born days met anybody so set on giving back money she's earned fair and square," Marcia wailed for the tenth time in as many days. She was hovering in the doorway of Lisa's room, dozens of slave bracelets jangling on the arms she flung up in a dramatic gesture of patent disgust. "You've been a nut case ever since you got back from the Eskimos, you know that?"

Lisa ignored her and calmly finished lacing up a new pair of runners.

"We need the bread more than Moneybags Morgan does, Leece," Marcia continued. "Be real. I mean, we've got bills to pay—"

"We've also got principles, Marcia," Lisa said with finality. "Or should have, anyway."

She got up off the floor and pulled a windbreaker out of the closet. After stuffing her arms into the sleeves, she scooped her backpack up off the futon, draped it over one shoulder and pushed past Marcia out of the room. "Morgan has finally returned from Oregon and California. The money goes back right now."

Lisa's appointment with Dan Morgan was for one o'clock. That left some fifteen minutes for her promised visit with John Turner at the security office.

On her way up the series of escalators to the fifth floor, she was struck yet again by the impracticality of security's location. She had said as much to Dan soon after he had assumed the reins of the store, just as she had made her opinions on the subject known to the Old Man more than once before that.

Like his father, Dan had listened politely but with the look that said, "Things've been this way for as long as we've *had* a security department."

Aloud he had said he appreciated her concern and suggestion and would take it under advisement. Which, Lisa was savvy enough to know, meant he wouldn't give the matter another thought.

Oh, well, Lisa thought with a mental shrug as she glided upward to fourth, it wasn't her problem anymore.

She spotted Jim Beenus behind a pillar, walkie-talkie to mouth; and over in the corner in China, Nick, the young clerk she'd pressed into service, what—three months ago?—was dusting a tall crystal vase. She waved a greeting, thinking, three months? Was that all the time that had passed since Dan Morgan made his stylish entrance into her ragged life?

She felt as though she had known him forever.

The realization oddly warmed and disturbed her. How could she feel so...close to a man who was—had been—no more than her employer and, as often as not, a thorn in her side? She had no answer to that question, only knew that she...*liked* him. Quite a bit. Their confrontation in Anchorage had hurt more than anything had hurt in the past. And mostly because she knew she had hurt him with her throwaway announcement of her plans to quit.

She was here today not only to return the money she hadn't earned and felt she didn't deserve, she also wanted to offer an apology once again. It was ironic how often she, who couldn't stand apologies, had apologized to this one man. And it was strange how little that fact rankled.

Still deep in thought, Lisa walked through the monitor room into the adjacent larger office and froze. A chorus of "Surprise!" nearly deafened her.

She stood and stared without comprehension at a dozen beaming faces beneath a canopy of colorful balloons. She saw two desks pushed together and loaded with food, a huge bowl of punch and towers of cups. And, off to the side, she saw John Turner and...Dan Morgan.

Lisa's bewildered gaze came to rest on his smiling one in a mute question that was immediately answered by John's call of "Party time. All you guys on break, stick around. Everyone else, back to work. The goodies'll be here all day even if Lisa won't."

About two-thirds of the room's occupants filed past her, bestowing friendly claps on the shoulder and teasing asides as they did.

Lisa, dazed, smiled at them all.

"Get your buns over here, guest of honor," Jonn called out to her. "Some of us working stiffs are starving."

Lisa swept another incredulous glance toward the array of multihued balloons bouncing gently against the low and dingy ceiling, and at the table filled with potluck dishes everyone had brought from home. Next to the punch sat a sheet cake slathered in pink-and-white icing with the words, GOODBYE AND GOOD LUCK inscribed in chocolate.

She took it all in, looked back at Dan and, for the first time in nearly twenty years, burst into tears.

Both men immediately rushed over to her, but it was John who gently folded her into his arms and awkwardly patted her back.

Lisa raised streaming eyes through which a tremulous smile was emerging. "I'm sorry," she said. Her voice cracked and she gave a self-conscious little laugh. "I don't usually do this. It's just—" She swallowed. "Nobody's ever thrown me a party before."

"It's okay, honey," John said gruffly. "You're a woman. You're entitled to spill a few tears...."

"Oh, John." His well-meant bit of chauvinism made Lisa laugh through her sniffles. She drew out of his embrace, taking care to avoid Dan Morgan's eyes though she was excruciatingly aware that he was watching her closely. She slipped her backpack off her shoulder and set it onto the floor, then searched her windbreaker pockets for a tissue.

A snowy handkerchief appeared at the edge of her peripheral vision. Unable to come up with a tissue of her own, she hesitantly accepted it.

"Uh...th-thanks," she said, forced by good manners to meet Dan's somber gaze before burying her face in the pristine softness of his—oh, Lord, was this silk?—hanky.

Did tears leave stains? she wondered with a touch of hysteria. Dare she actually blow her nose in it? She'd have to have it dry-cleaned...

Gingerly dabbing at her eyes, she elected to noisily snuffle through her nose in an effort to reverse its flow rather than soil the expensive cloth.

Suddenly it was taken out of her hand and pressed to her nostrils by a firm masculine hand. "Blow," Dan ordered matter-of-factly.

Lisa, feeling about three years old, blew.

After he'd wiped her as efficiently as a mother, Dan folded the square and carelessly stuffed it back into his pocket.

"Please let me—"

"Maria'll take care of it," he cut short Lisa's protest.

"Punch?" A cup of red liquid appeared out of nowhere.

Lisa accepted the drink from John and offered a tremulous smile to both men. "Thank you," she said, and they all knew she meant more than just the hanky and the punch.

"Doesn't this food look good?" Dan said heartily, rubbing his hands in a great show of anticipation and thus terminating a potentially awkward and emotional pause. "Personally, I've had my eyes on that great-smelling chili ever since I got here."

"I made that," John declared, joining Lisa and Dan in the short line at the makeshift buffet. "Guaranteed to cure whatever ails you."

"As I remember from a barbecue last summer," Lisa chimed in, "what he means is it'll burn out any and all hostile organisms in your system. Unfortunately, every friendly one, too."

Dan chuckled. John, as expected, loudly protested.

"Slander. Lies. It's a little hot, that's all." He eyed askance the cautious helping Dan had taken. "Don't let her scare you off, boss."

"Oh?" Dan shot Lisa a look from beneath raised brows before he said, "I've found it's best to be careful when things get hot."

"Makes life dull, doesn't it?" John added garlic bread and vegetables from a relish tray to his laden plate.

"Think so?" Dan's eyes met Lisa's again, and their expression told her he was not thinking of the chili as he slowly added, "You could be right."

A surge of tingling emotion shot up Lisa's legs to settle uneasily in her stomach. She took her time selecting minuscule helpings from the assortment of salads and casseroles. Moments ago she had been hungry, now she doubted she could swallow even a single bite. What had his look and his words meant?

And, more to the point, what did she want them to mean?

Her feet dragged as she went to join John and Dan by the window. Right then she would have vastly preferred some solitude in which to ponder the questions that were plaguing her. But this was a party....

She stuck a bright smile onto her face and a forkful of food into her mouth.

"How's school?" John asked.

"Ugh." Lisa groaned through a mouthful of unwanted potato salad. She rolled her eyes in a don't-ask expression. What with exams, her thesis and related lab work, things were rough.

"Anchorage set you back a lot, didn't it?" Dan had been bothered by this and it showed. "I know that this assignment—"

"Hey, John, can you come here a minute." One of the agents on duty had stuck his head into the room and was calling out to John.

"Excuse me." With a grimace, he jogged away.

Left to themselves, Dan and Lisa were silent for a moment, though neither ate. Then they both spoke in unison.

"Look, about Anchorage—"

"Dan, I want to apologize—"

Both broke off. They exchanged chagrined glances. Dan cleared his throat.

"I was going to say that I know the assignment in Anchorage greatly inconvenienced you. And I'm sure you're studying day and night now to make up for it. I wish you'd tell me if there's anything I can do."

"I would, and there isn't. Look, it's not that bad," Lisa hastened to assure him. She tried for humor. "I do get to sleep about four hours a night."

"Lisa—"

"Just kidding. I'm doing fine. It's just as well, though, that I don't work here anymore."

"Oh?" Dan set his nearly untouched plate aside. "I'm glad things worked out for the best then."

"They did." Lisa grabbed at the opening. "Except that I wish I'd been a little more timely and tactful in the way I told you of my plans to quit and—" She held up a hand when Dan seemed about to interrupt. "And I can't take the extra pay you included in my last paycheck."

"Why not?" Dan's brows snapped into their customary frown as he added, "No, don't bother to answer that. It's charity, right?"

"Right."

"Lisa, that's—"

"That's the way it is, Mr. Morgan." Lisa, too, put her plate aside. She went to get her pack and pulled an envelope from its outer pocket.

"I had to cash the check in order to take out the amount I did earn. Here's the rest."

She held it out to Dan, who glared at it before, with an explosive sigh, almost snatching it from her.

"Someday I'm going to win one of these confrontations of ours," he promised her darkly.

Lisa's grin was a shade wobbly. "I'm afraid our battle days are over, Mr. Morgan." She made a project of resettling her pack on the floor against the wall before lifting her gaze to his. "Now that I'm no longer a Morgan's employee, I doubt we'll have occasion to see each other again."

God, she was going to miss him, she thought with only a touch of surprise. Her eyes dropped to Dan's lips and lingered there. They looked firm and arrogant, those lips, compressed as they were just then in a severe line. But—oh, they'd been soft and ever so exciting when they had pressed against her own. Caressed her own. Devoured her own . . .

She swallowed against the sudden dryness of her mouth and forced her eyes upward only to find her memories mirrored in the turbulance of Dan's gaze. Everyone, everything else in the room, receded as they shared once more the tempestuous emotions their kiss in Anchorage had aroused.

It was Dan who looked away first. Making a study of the ebony gleam of his loafers, he buried his hands deep in his pockets. "I, uh—"

He cleared his throat and raised his eyes to Lisa's. "I'd like to see you again, Lisa. To hear how you're doing," he hurried to add. "How about dinner some night soon?"

"D-dinner?" Lisa stumbled over the word as if it were a foreign one. Her reaction perversely put Dan at ease.

"Yes, dinner," he said with amusement quirking at the corners of his mouth. "As in food. You know—" He gestured toward some of the other agents attacking heaped plates. "Eating."

"Oh." Lisa laughed in spite of the sense of shock she still felt. "*That* kind of dinner."

She sobered, biting her lip as she tried to sort out all the possible implications of Dan's invitation. A date was what he was asking for, she told herself. Men and women who were attracted to each other were known to go out on dates. . . .

Was she attracted to Dan Morgan? Oh, yes. But dates led to kisses. Kisses led to . . .

Was she ready for the kind of commitment she knew kisses between Dan and herself would inevitably lead to?

"I had no idea my invitation would cause you such agony," Dan said, a trifle miffed.

"I'm sorry." Lisa shook her head and tried for a smile. "It's not that I don't appreciate your asking. I just don't think it'd be a good idea to—you know, see each other after this."

"Why not?"

"I just don't. My life and yours are—" she shrugged, feeling cornered and not liking it "—incompatible. Things just wouldn't work."

Perhaps because he had thought the same thing more than once, Dan impatiently challenged Lisa's words. "Can you give me one good reason why you feel that way?"

"No," Lisa admitted, "I used to think I could but I probably can't. Still, I know I'm right. You and I, Mr. Morgan, are from different worlds. We simply don't match."

"Okay, folks, gather around." John came back into the room, pushing a dolly with two large gift-wrapped cartons on it. "Lisa, Mr. Morgan, would you come over here please. Let 'em through, kids. That's it, thank you."

He beamed at Lisa, placing an arm around her shoulders and pulling her against his side.

"We're losing a fantastic agent here today," he said to the room at large. "A hard worker and a good friend to us all."

Muted cheers, big smiles and applause followed. Lisa's sorely overtaxed emotions took a swing toward nostalgia.

"Morgan's loss is Misotec's—and Lisa's—gain, though. We wish her well in the new career she worked so long and hard to attain."

More applause.

Lisa sniffed and once more accepted Dan's proffered handkerchief.

"Lisa—" John squeezed her shoulders, then released them and grinned down at her as he said, "As a token of our esteem we present you with your very own personal . . . Computer!"

About an hour later Lisa was on the escalator going down. She had a lab session to attend but knew she wouldn't be able to keep her thoughts on track. Still, at this point in time she couldn't afford to play hookey, either.

Her heart was heavy in spite of the joy over the computer that would be delivered to her apartment. She was leaving a large part of herself behind here at Morgan's. The security staff had been an extended family of sorts, the job itself more than just a source of income.

And then there was, first, last and always, Dan Morgan.

There had been no chance to get back to their interrupted conversation before he'd had to rush off to some meeting or other. Before he left, he'd been rather quiet and had kept in the background during the presentation of her going-away present. And leaving, he had merely shaken her hand and said as to some stranger, "Best of luck to you."

Guess he agrees we don't match, she thought sadly—and the next moment almost pitched headlong onto her face as some guy in a hurry ruthlessly shoved her down the last three steps of the escalator. She had barely regained her balance when Bob Janssen stormed past her toward the store's main entrance. An inadvertent swipe of his brawny arm had her tottering again.

Three years on the job had put Lisa's reflexes on automatic. The fact that she no longer worked for Morgan's forgotten, Lisa joined the chase.

Outside on the sidewalk, Janssen and the suspect were arguing, shoving. Without hesitation, Lisa marched up to them.

"Hold it," she said sharply, startling both men. They stared at her, breathing hard but momentarily motionless. Lisa glanced at Bob. "Need help?"

"Grab my cuffs," he panted, renewing his efforts to catch the man's flailing arms. "This guy's trouble."

Lisa hastened to unhook the handcuffs from the back of Janssen's belt and danced around trying to clamp them on the suspect's elusive wrists.

"Have you called for backup?" she asked, breathless from her exertions to get hold of an arm.

"Yes, but—"

Bob's answer was cut short when, without warning, the man freed himself from their precarious hold. He kneed Janssen in the groin. With a guttural moan Bob doubled over, clutching himself.

Before Lisa could even think to lend aid in any way, the suspect had one arm around her neck in a stranglehold. As if by magic, a switchblade knife appeared in his hand.

A cry escaped Lisa's lips before she could compress them. A sharp jerk of the arm at her throat stifled the small sound and cut off her breath.

Janssen's head snapped up. Wide-eyed, he and Lisa stared at each other. Neither dared to make a move, for pressed now against Lisa's right temple was the needle-sharp tip of the knife.

Chapter Eight

Now then, little lady," the man holding the knife at Lisa's head wheezed into her ear, "let's get out of here. Make a move," he warned Bob Janssen, still in a crouch at their feet, "and she gets it."

Slowly he began to walk backward and away. He pulled Lisa along in the crook of his arm and completely ignored the passersby who, incredibly, did no more than shuffle out of the way and gape. Some twenty feet from the cluster of spectators, the man lowered the knife and increased his pace.

As if emerging from a trance, Lisa began to struggle. She clawed at the arm that all but strangled her, all the while racking her brain for a self-defense technique that would free her. If only she could manage a decent grip, maybe she'd be able to toss her assailant off.

Damn—it was no use. The man's sleeve was bulky leather and her fingers found no purchase. Frustrated and enraged now more than scared, she kicked out with her feet in hopes of striking a shin. Anything.

"Let go of me, you creep," she screamed hoarsely. "Bob! Help! Daaaniel!"

The hand with the knife was clamped roughly over her mouth, cutting off breath and voice. It also reminded her that the man was armed. And dangerous. For now she'd be smart just to go along.

The man began to run now, never easing his grip on Lisa. His hold forced her to stumble along at his side or be dragged. They stopped at the fence that enclosed a construction site in the block next to Morgan's. Work on the project had been halted by a strike several weeks ago, and the future high rise loomed before them like some huge and barren stack of concrete blocks.

They skirted it, searching for a way inside, and came upon a gate in the fence. The lock gave beneath the force of one well-placed kick. Lisa was shoved ahead and through. Tripping over her own feet, she fell to the ground. Before she could even think of getting up, she was lifted by the scruff of her windbreaker and force-trotted toward the skeleton building.

They ran inside, their footsteps producing a muffled, eerie echo in the murky, cavernous interior. Somewhere in its center they came upon a haphazard stack of concrete blocks. The man scrambled up onto the pile and dragged Lisa after him. He let go of her neck, but she had no time to draw a breath of relief. She was grabbed around the waist and hoisted overhead and up onto a steel girder. She lay across it like a sack of cement, panting, arms and legs dangling.

"Get up," her captor's harsh voice ordered from below. "Move it."

Lisa hastened to obey. Ruthlessly squelching her childhood fear of heights, she wriggled herself around and straddled the beam.

"Get up, I said. Move, move." The man glanced nervously back over his shoulder before reaching up to haul himself onto the steel support after her. "Keep moving," he ordered.

Cautiously, on hands and knees, Lisa inched forward along the girder as fast as she dared. She fully expected at any moment to lose her balance and crash to the ground some ten feet below. She could hear her captor's ragged breathing at her heels, could smell his fear. Or was that her own?

At last she reached a pillar and could go no further.

"Okay. Now turn around and sit."

Lisa squeezed her eyes shut, took a deep breath and willed her limbs to obey. Straddling the beam again, she gingerly worked herself around until she sat facing her captor. Her back was propped against the pillar, giving her support and an illusion of security. It was instantly dispelled when she raised her eyes.

The shoplifter was standing right in front of her. His wickedly glinting steel blade seemed like an extension of the hand that was only inches away from her face.

"Now you hear me good, little girl," he rasped with deadly menace, bending to wave the knife slowly back and forth beneath her nose. "You keep real quiet, and don't make no sudden moves, and just maybe you won't get hurt."

He reeked of stale tobacco and sweat. His hand shook as he pressed the tip of the knife against her cheek. Just hard enough to prick the skin. "Know what I mean?"

Lisa felt blood trickle warmly down the side of her face. She blinked her eyes *yes*, not daring to nod. Her throat worked, but there was nothing to swallow. She was at this man's mercy, she thought with despair, precariously perched on a foot-wide chunk of steel with a knife stuck in her face.

She was helpless.

The word rankled. Resentment stiffened her backbone. Only for now, she sternly reminded herself. She was helpless only for now. She grimly blinked *yes* once more.

The man's satisfied smirk was a grimace of evil in the twilight between them. But he pulled back the knife and straightened away from her.

Lisa's chin sagged onto her chest. Relief made her tremble, and she clutched the sides of the girder to steady herself. A quick downward glance proved to be a mistake. In the gathering darkness of late afternoon, the ground had disappeared yet seemed to draw her like a magnet. She jerked her head up.

"Hey. No tricks," she was immediately warned again.

"N-no," she choked out. "Can I pull my legs up?"

Taking his grunt as assent, Lisa carefully pulled her quaking limbs onto the beam and against her chest. She wrapped her arms tightly around them, then slowly lowered her chin onto her knees.

For a few moments she just sat like that, marshaling her inner resources. When she felt steadier, she drew a deep breath and looked toward her captor.

He had lowered himself to the beam a couple of feet away, straddling the steel support and facing her. He had placed the knife in the small space between them. Its sharp tip pointed toward her, a tangible reminder of the precarious situation she was in.

Lisa needed no reminder.

She shivered. It was cold and drafty on their perch, but she forced herself to ignore the discomfort and to concentrate on the man in front of her. He was in his early thirties, she guessed, looking him over as carefully as the fading light allowed. Thin to the point of gauntness. Dressed in jeans, black turtleneck sweater and a scuffed leather flyer's jacket. Strands of brownish hair stuck out from beneath a black knitted cap. A brownish stubble shadowed hollow cheeks and a pointed chin.

He lit a cigarette and Lisa watched, fascinated, as he dragged in a lungful of smoke before forcefully expelling it to extinguish the tiny flame of the match. Their gazes clashed as he did so. Apparently pleased by something he read in Lisa's eyes, the man barked a short laugh.

Lisa shivered again. She hugged her legs more tightly against her body.

"Why are you doing this?" she demanded in a hoarse whisper. "Why are you keeping me here? You're only making things worse for yo—"

"Shut up."

She could smell more than see him lean closer. The rapidly encroaching darkness had reduced him to a murky silhouette. She could hear the clink of metal as he picked up the knife and hissed, "If you don't want that pretty face of yours messed up, you better can the conversation, lady. I'm trying to think."

Lisa shrank back against her pillar as if to merge with it. Her hands were lumps of ice locked around her knees in a death grip. She willed them to relax, then slowly draw apart and slide into her jacket pockets.

In one of them her fingers brushed against something soft. Dan Morgan's handkerchief. She had kept it when Dan had lent it to her a second time, when the computer had been presented to her at the party. Could that really have been only a few short hours ago? She felt as if some giant hand had in the meantime plucked her out of a life she controlled and dumped her onto a nightmare runaway train of events.

Where was Dan right now? she wondered. What was he doing? And what would he think when he heard about the mess she had gotten herself into this time? Would he worry? Would he be mad?

She closed her fist around the silken cloth and carefully drew it out of the pockets. Yes, he'd be worried. And, yes, he'd be angry.

Because he cared?

Lisa pressed her face into the handkerchief, inhaled Dan's scent. His features materialized in front of her like magic. He was smiling at her tenderly, the way he had smiled after he had kissed her in Anchorage. And she thought with a soblike catch in her breath that, yes, he cared. Or used to.

Something caught at Lisa's heart and squeezed. Something cold and relentless. Fear. Not the kind she had been feeling all along, trapped on this girder, but a different, more devastating kind that came with the realization that she might never see Daniel Morgan again.

For the first time since the man had grabbed her in front of the store, hot tears welled up in her eyes.

Dan exited I-5 and followed the flow of traffic toward the downtown core. He was headed back to the store after spending most of the afternoon at a stuffy chamber of commerce meeting. Afterward he had gone out for dinner and, though it was well after closing, planned to work for several hours yet that night. The time away in Anchorage, Portland and L.A. had put him in arrears on his paperwork. In order to get caught up, he'd be burning a lot of midnight oil the next couple of days.

As he drove along Denny Way, his thoughts were not on his work, however. Instead they were replaying the tête-à-tête he had had with Lisa earlier that day at her party. He was giving their exchange a variety of different endings. Ultimately, though, he always got back to Lisa's emphatic, "We don't match."

And he had to admit in some ways they didn't. Ways that seemed unimportant to him but obviously mattered to Lisa. His social position, for instance. Without coming out and actually saying so, Lisa's attitude had often enough implied she thought him and the things he represented stuffy and self-serving. His relative wealth seemed to be an even bigger stumbling block.

And while they hadn't gotten around to fighting about politics as yet, he would bet his favorite golf shoes that, given time and opportunity, they certainly would. In fact, now that he thought of it, it would be something to look forward to.

So they didn't match. Big deal. Where was it written that people had to share the same background and philosophy in order to be compatible? What about the old "opposites attract" adage?

Take his parents. His mother had been a penniless clerk in a bakeshop when the Old Man had fallen in love with her. And she hadn't done at all badly as the wife of one of Seattle's leading citizens.

Wife. Was that what he meant for Lisa Hanrahan to become—his wife?

The notion so startled Dan, he wrenched the steering wheel sharply to the right. He swore as the front tire of his silver-gray Mercedes sedan bounced against the concrete divider and thus initiated another swerve in the opposite direction. A quick, sheepish glance in the rearview mirror reassured him his inattentiveness had not created undue havoc for any other drivers.

He relaxed and allowed his thoughts to drift back to the word that had sneaked up and electrified his reflexes.

Wife. Up until a second ago, he had never thought about any woman in that context. And Lisa Hanrahan least of all. To be honest, he hadn't thought beyond the exquisite pleasure of reclaiming the sweetness of her lips and of awakening the passion he had felt in her. Nor had he thought beyond the fact that now she no longer worked for him, he would be free to pursue those pleasures and . . . more.

An affair. Was that what he had planned?

At that, a wry chuckle lightened his brooding frown. *He* might well be planning to have an affair with her, but the Lisa Hanrahan he had come to know and appreciate would squash that notion like a bug.

Envisioning the scene—her pink-faced outrage, flaming gypsy eyes and scathing choice of words—brought a smile of anticipation to his lips. It still lingered as he made a left turn onto Second Avenue, which brought him within two blocks of his store.

Traffic was at a standstill just a few yards ahead, and farther up the street he could see the reason why. Red and blue lights were flashing everywhere. Swell.

Unable to go on, Dan impatiently wrenched open his door and got out for a better look. Just as he'd thought, police units, some fire trucks and an ambulance were clustered in front of...

Dan craned his neck and blinked to be sure he was seeing right. Alarm bells went off in his head. Why, most of the vehicles were right in front of Morgan's! Something was happening at his store. Something *bad*.

An unnamed dread was like a fist suddenly clutching his gut. His heart did a funny kind of somersault before settling into a rapid and irregular beat. He cast a quick glance around for a way out, saw that his car was well and truly blocked in and, without further thought, leaned down to kill the engine. He yanked out the keys, slammed the door and was running.

"You, inside the building. This is the police. We have you surrounded. Come out with your hands up."

As the first words echoed around them, both people inside the skeleton high rise snapped to attention.

Incredibly, Lisa had been dozing, she didn't know for how long. Her eyelids popped open. It took a moment of sightless staring to remember where she was and how she had gotten there. Gradually it sank in that it wasn't dark anymore. Giant, glaring beacons of light crisscrossed and collided, creating more brightness than the sun ever could. Pillars and cross beams cast long pick-up-sticks kinds of shadows everywhere.

One of those shadows still had Lisa and her captor swallowed up.

Her captor. Lisa's gaze flew to the man with whom she shared this murky end of a steel girder some dozen feet off the ground. He was crouching a scant foot away from her, the knife clutched in an upraised hand. She saw him twist his upper torso this way and that as if trying to locate and face down the magnified, disembodied voice that warned them once again to give up and come out.

With the man's attention thus diverted, Lisa acted purely on instinct. While both of her hands clutched the girder's edges for support, she lifted her feet and jerked her legs tightly against her chest on one sharply sucked-in breath. Then, concentrating all her energies into her legs, she forcefully kicked out.

"Aiii—yeh!" The sound of her yell mingled with the thunk of her sneakered feet connecting solidly with the side of the man's head. Both seemed to reverberate all the way up her shins. The impact knocked her captor off balance and sideways off his perch. She whooped again.

As he fell, though, arms flailing, one of his hands groped in the air for something solid to latch onto. It made a grab for the leg of Lisa's jeans, missed, then closed like the jaws of a vise around her foot.

Lisa felt a mighty yank. Instead of holding on, she threw up her hands to counteract the sudden loss of balance. And then she too was falling.

They landed with a thud in a tangled heap on compacted dirt. Something snapped in Lisa's right arm, caught at a funny angle beneath her body as it hit the ground. She clenched her teeth. She shut her eyes tightly but couldn't stop scalding tears from welling up in automatic response to the excruciating pain.

Struggling to catch her breath, only dimly aware of yet another blaring message from the bullhorn, Lisa lay unmoving for long pain-filled moments. Her nose and mouth were pressed into the dirt. Her lower body was sprawled half on top of the man's, their legs were oddly entangled.

Carefully, eyes blinking to clear bothersome tears and adjust to the light, Lisa lifted her head and craned around for a look at him. He lay perfectly still, flat on his back. As far as she could make out, his eyes were closed. His face seemed ghostly white against the dirt. His knife was nowhere in sight.

Was he unconscious, or...?

Lisa resolutely refused to dwell on the *or*. She had to get away while she could.

She struggled to sit up, clenched her teeth against a gasp. Her arm! It had to be broken.

Ruthlessly forcing herself to concentrate on the business at hand, Lisa rolled over and freed the injured limb she had lain on. Rather than give relief, the removal of her weight caused the pain to increase a hundredfold.

She strove to ignore it, scrambled awkwardly onto one knee, tried to stand. Tears rushed unheeded down icy cheeks; a choking sob escaped her.

On her feet at last, she paused a moment, weaving like a drunk, and gathered her strength. She cast a quick glance toward the man. He had not moved. She told herself not to worry about him, to just get out as quickly as she could.

Cradling the injured arm close to her body, she slowly began to walk. Her legs shook but she willed them to move forward. One step, the next—don't fall. Keep going. After what seemed like an eternity, she stumbled out into the open.

"Help," she croaked, dropping to her knees. Indistinct figures rushed toward her. Pain and reaction threatened to overwhelm her. Someone scooped her up. As if from a great distance she heard an urgently voiced question.

"Where's the guy who took you?"

"Inside," she mumbled. "The middle . . ."

Whoever was holding her shifted her weight in his arms. A lightning streak of pain shot up her arm. She cried out. And then, mercifully, knew only blackness and crazy dreams.

She awoke once. Dan was there, holding one of her hands. They were in a vehicle, and she was in some kind of bed.

"Where . . . ?"

"In an ambulance. You'll be fine."

"Is . . . is he dead?" she asked. Her mind was so fuzzy, and it was so much work just to talk.

Dan seemed to know who she meant, though. He shook his head. "No." He squeezed her fingers reassuringly. "He's alive and on his way to the hospital, just as you are."

"What . . ."

"Shh," Dan said so softly she could barely hear him. "Don't worry about him. Worry about you." He might have said something else, but by then it was too much trouble to listen. Sleep reclaimed her.

During the time since their arrival at the hospital, Dan had been condemned to helplessly linger and wait. It had given him ample opportunity to think. Over and over he had relived the horror of seeing Lisa's seemingly lifeless body carried out from behind that construction fence. Guilt was flaying him like a bullwhip.

Why, he asked himself time and again, why hadn't he moved the security office to the first floor as she had so often suggested? Help might have reached Janssen—and her—in time then.

She could have been killed. The horrifying thought was accompanied by intense self-loathing. While he had sat, safe and sound, in a hotel banquet room, Lisa Hanrahan—all five-feet-nothing of her—had been struggling on Morgan's behalf with a desperate criminal. She had courageously defended *his* property; property that she would never believe meant much less to him than she did.

She had risked her life and limb for him—and for a company she no longer even worked for.

And what had he been doing? After spending hours expounding business generalities with his cronies, he had dined on Dungeness crab and mentally devised ways of luring Lisa Hanrahan into his bed.

Just then Dan could not think of a name low enough to call himself, and he dreaded having to face her. Still, not to see her would be infinitely worse.

Lifelong training enabled an outward calm to mask the volcano of emotions just waiting to erupt inside of him as he quietly stepped into the private room he had insisted Lisa be given. Her stay at the hospital would be brief—a couple of days of observation.

On arrival she had rallied just long enough to tell everyone within earshot that she had no insurance and that all she needed was to have her arm put in a cast. No overnight stay; she was fine.

Dan knew she would be furious on finding out she had been overruled.

The room was quiet. Dan gingerly tiptoed up to the bed and risked a peek.

Lisa was still asleep, her face turned slightly into the pillow. Her hair was a riot of dark waves and curls that emphasized the pallor of her skin. Her long black lashes lay like a fringe on the ivory satin of her skin, skin now stained by fatigue just below their upturned tips. A rectangle of adhesive tape was like an obscene brand on her downy cheek.

Dan's eyes drank her in. His heart ached with the knowledge that he could do nothing to ease her pain though he would willingly cut off his own arm if only it would help. He vowed that she would lack for nothing throughout her convalescence.

Gently he trailed a fingertip across the back of the deceptively delicate hand, then bent and tenderly kissed her on the mouth.

Lisa stirred, not sure what had awakened her, though she imagined it had probably been some gossamer wings batting at her lips. In her dream she had been in a meadow, a child again, chasing butterflies....

She reluctantly opened her eyes to the reality of Dan Morgan's troubled deep blue gaze just inches away. And she knew then that he, not butterfly wings, must have kissed and awakened her.

Daniel Morgan. Her very own Prince Charm— Wait a minute...what was he doing in her bedroom?

Memory returned all in a rush. She knew where she was. In the hospital!

Lisa's lids popped all the way open. She started to raise her head, but needle-sharp stabs of pain at her temples turned the heated protest she had meant to make into a shuddering moan. She strove to stifle the sound by biting her lip. Her head subsided limply back into the pillow.

At this latest evidence of her suffering, Dan snapped upright and away. "I didn't mean to disturb you," he said, guilt and frustration making him sound gruff and formal. "I just wanted to make sure you have everything you need."

Lisa stared up at him, frowned at his tone. The notion that moments before, those sternly compressed lips might actually have kissed her seemed suddenly ludicrous. Dan was clearly angry.

Well, she was plenty angry herself.

"Why am I in the hospital?" she demanded as forcefully as she was able. "Didn't I make it clear—"

"You did," Dan interrupted. "But the doctors had other ideas, for which I'm glad. You need rest."

"I can rest at home, and a lot more cheaply."

"Forget about that, will you?" In the face of her obstinacy, Dan found it a struggle to keep his tone moderate. "So, how do you feel?"

"Lousy." She sniffed. "My head hurts."

"Concussion." Dan reached out and placed a hand on her brow. "You're hot. Why don't I call the nurse so she can give you something?"

"No." Lisa gave a small shudder. His hand on her forehead was gently soothing and quite at odds with the forbidding expression on his face. "I'm still nauseous from the stuff they administered in the ambulance. Besides, I read they charge something like a dollar for just an aspirin in places like this."

"You're not to worry about that."

"But I do," Lisa said flatly, adding with a frown, "You must be tired. Why don't you go home?"

Dan straightened, withdrawing his hand. He shrugged. "I can't deny that I'm tired, but I'll stay a bit, if you don't mind."

"I do mind. Go home. I'll be fine."

"Of course you'll be fine." Dan cautioned himself to ignore her ungracious attitude. She was hurt and hurting. Her precious pride was dented. If sniping at him made her feel better, he could take it. He attempted a soothing smile, but it withered almost immediately at Lisa's next charge.

"You're angry, aren't you?"

"No. I—"

"Don't deny it, it's written all over you." Lisa's eyes blazed like black coals in her pale face. "So just spit it out. Tell me I should have stayed out of things. Tell me I should have left poor Janssen to his own devices, that at most I should have called for help. Tell me I should've done anything, anything at all, except get myself embroiled in another fiasco. Tell me!"

"No," Dan said quietly, almost sadly. None of the things she was charging him with had occurred to him at all. He had been too busy worrying about Lisa's well-being and his own culpability in this sorry mess to even think of recriminations. It hurt, learning she thought him so unfeeling. So self-serving. And the hurt in turn fueled his own anger.

"Now that you've brought it up, though," he said in a deliberately icy drawl, "it *would* interest me to know what, if anything, you were thinking as you forged into battle like an amazon?"

"There was no time to think. I just—"

"Ah, yes." Dan crossed his arms over his chest and nodded. "Of course. Act first, think second, and to hell with the consequences. The familiar Hanrahan motto."

"Oh! Of all the ungrateful..." Outrage choked her.

Dan was quick to take advantage. "Not ungrateful at all, Miss Hanrahan. On the contrary, Morgan's is most willing to pay their debts. You'll be compensated for your trouble, and—just for the record—your medical bills will be paid, as well."

"No." Lisa's tone, though it had not risen above a fierce whisper, brooked no contradiction. "I don't want your money, do you hear me? I no longer work for Morgan's. They, *you*, owe me nothing."

Their eyes fought on long after the words had stopped. In the end, Dan admitted defeat—or, at least, seemed to—by lowering his gaze to the cast on Lisa's arm. As he stared at it, the little muscles above his jaw jumped in agitation. His Adam's apple bobbed as he worked at swallowing the heated arguments he still longed to shout at her stubbornness.

"I'm sorry," was all he said when he finally trusted himself to speak. "This isn't the time or the place to discuss these things."

"Nor will there be a better time or place, Mr. Morgan. Our association is over. I'd prefer if you left me alone. I'll take care of myself the way I always have."

"Is that really how you want it, Lisa?"

Dan raised his eyes and gazed into Lisa's for long, heart-stopping moments. Like a thief in sudden daylight, her anger wanted to flee when confronted by the expression of pain and regret she saw on his face.

She could not look away; yet she couldn't change her mind and say she didn't mean it, either. She loathed charity—especially his.

"Yes," she whispered past the constriction in her throat. "That's how I want it."

"Well, then," Dan said, feeling awkward, hurt and an overwhelming need to be gone. He backed away from the bed, half lifting one hand in a parting gesture. "Take care of yourself."

He retreated a few steps more, hesitated. When Lisa still did not speak, he gave a short nod and turned away.

John Turner was standing in the doorway, but Dan brushed past him without a word.

"What's got him so riled?" John asked, staring after Dan.

He had to repeat the question before he got an answer.

"Me," Lisa told him in a tiny voice. She expelled a long, tremulous breath and sniffed into the silk handkerchief she had refused to surrender. Never in her life had she felt worse than she did at that moment.

But then, she thought with bitter insight and regret, she had never been in love before.

Chapter Nine

John looked bewildered as he sauntered further into the room. That night he and Dan Morgan had kept a joint vigil outside the emergency room while Lisa's injuries were being treated. The worry they had shared had created a sort of bond between the two men that transcended the amiable working relationship they already had. John's respect for Dan had grown into a genuine liking.

The look on Dan's face when he had stormed out of Lisa's room moments before brought to mind another occasion some months ago. It had been on one of Dan Morgan's first couple of days at the store and, as best as John could recollect, the sassy party currently pulling a long face in this very hospital bed had been responsible for the explosion then, too.

And here he thought those two had begun to really hit it off.

John swallowed a disgusted grunt, stopping at the foot of the bed to contemplate its gloomy occupant for a charged moment or two. He was thinking that going for that cup of coffee and giving Dan some time alone with Lisa probably had not been the best idea he'd ever had.

"Now don't tell me," he drawled, his tone dry as desert sand. "Let me guess." He took his time coming around to the side of the bed, forefinger tapping the bridge of his nose as if he were deep in thought. "You didn't like something Morgan said and, bingo—you two had a fight."

"Sort of."

Lisa knew it sounded silly, put like that, yet that's how most of her confrontations with Dan Morgan seemed to have happened. With him always wanting to take charge, always assuming she needed help or something only he or his money could provide. And with her always on the defensive, trying to convince him of her abilities, scrapping to protect her pride and independence.

And now she had gone and fallen in love with the man! How in the world could that have happened? He wasn't anything like the ideal man she had envisioned for herself.

She had always imagined—when she took the time to contemplate such things at all—that the man of her choice, her true love, would be someone of just ordinary looks and average dimensions. Someone deep and perhaps brooding; someone who thought, *really* thought, about the state of the world. Someone who was involved in bettering it.

In other words, someone not at all like Daniel Morgan who, besides being tall, well built and much too handsome, was athletic and had a sense of humor. Yet, she could have reconciled herself to those things. What really gave her trouble was the fact that he belonged to a class of people she considered to be shallow and egocentric. Snobbish. People who, in her opinion, had no firsthand experience with hunger and deprivation but condescended to those who did.

People who talked of compensation and paying bills when what they should have done was hold and comfort the injured and confused person in this hospital bed.

Oh, Dan. Lisa turned her face toward the night-darkened window and caught sight of John Turner's incredulous face reflected in the glass.

"How could you two fight at a time like this?" he was asking.

"I don't know. I only said what had to be said. Namely that I won't take his handouts."

"Handouts, huh? What'd he do, offer to pay for this room?"

"Among other things."

"Why, the son of a bitch. Someone oughta grab the bum and whup his hide . . ."

"Don't." Lisa closed her eyes. "I'd just like to see how you'd feel in my shoes."

"Grateful," John said promptly. "And without insurance or available cash, so should you be. Besides, Lisa, the guy's crazy about you—"

"Ha!" She rolled her head back toward him. "He feels obligated because I got hurt for Morgan's, so to speak. But aside from that, what he feels for me is contempt for—as he put it—always acting first and thinking second."

"We-e-ell . . ."

"I don't need to hear that from you, too, John."

"Okay, but you will hear this. The man cares about you. He was tied up in twice as many knots as the twins and I were, and we really love you. God knows why," John added drolly, reaching out to squeeze her good hand.

"Oh, John." Lisa squeezed back. She wanted to cry, fought it, lost. With a wrenching sob, some dam inside her broke. Tears too rarely shed burst forth with awesome strength. Lisa tore her hand from John's and covered her eyes.

John was off the chair and perched on the edge of the bed in a flash. "Lisa. Leece, what're you doing?" he asked, too shocked and dismayed by her sobs to be bothered by the foolishness of his question. His hands hovered helplessly in the vicinity of her shoulders, not sure if he dared hold her or not. "What's the matter?"

"I don't kno-o-o-w...." Lisa wailed, looking at him with streaming eyes.

He settled his hands on her shoulders then and gently drew her up against his chest.

"Hush," he crooned, awkwardly stroking and patting. "Shhh. Hush now, hear? It'll be okay...."

"Oh, John, I'm so mixed up," Lisa mumbled, sniffing against the flow of tears. "Nothing's the way I thought it would be, you know? I thought if I got my degree and a terrific job, I'd be so happy. But now—" she half shrugged and sniffed again "—I don't know...."

"What is it, Leece?" John urged, "Tell me."

"I...I can't."

"Sure you can. Look at me." He nudged her with his shoulder until she lifted her head off his chest. "Is this about Dan Morgan?"

Lisa sucked in her lower lip to keep it from trembling. Another deluge of tears threatened to blind her again. Choking them back, she gave a shaky nod. "Y-yes."

John searched her eyes for long thoughtful moments. Neither he nor Lisa was aware that Marc and Marcia had come in minutes before and were standing, entranced, at the foot of the bed.

"You're in love with him," John pronounced, something like awe lowering his voice an octave. "Aren't you?"

A tear slowly rolled down Lisa's cheek as she squeezed her eyes shut and turned her face into his chest. John felt more than heard her muffled, "Yes."

"Oh, boy." He expelled an explosive breath and tilted his face toward the ceiling.

For quite a while no one spoke or moved. Lisa's occasional snuffle was the only sound in the room. And then she said in a tiny voice, "I want to go home."

John looked down at the tousled head still pressed against his chest. "You will," he soothed. "In just a day or so."

"No, I don't mean that," Lisa whispered. She pulled away to lift tear-drenched eyes to his and wailed, "I want my mom."

Pineville was blanketed by the season's first snow. Though it was only three days after Thanksgiving, it wasn't unusual for eastern Washington and the Cascades to get snow this early. Still, as Lisa and her mother crossed the large yard that separated Faith Church from the parsonage, Jeanne Hanrahan looked skyward with displeasure.

"I'm not at all sure I'm ready for this," she said, shivering. "It'll be a long winter."

Lisa made some indistinct sound of agreement. She too was cold. The fingertips hanging out from the end of her cast were rapidly turning numb. It had to be well below freezing, she figured, which was probably why the snow scrunched so noisily beneath their feet.

She had just attended Sunday worship, as she had on every one of the three Sundays she had spent with her parents. Just as she had attended Bible study again every Wednesday evening. As far as the Reverend Lucas Hanrahan was concerned, adulthood and prolonged absences from home made no difference whatever to what was right. Lisa and her brothers had attended these functions when they had lived here, and they would attend them when they visited, too.

Which was probably why those of her brothers and their families who had made it home for Thanksgiving had arrived on Thursday morning and departed Saturday afternoon.

Lucky them. Every Sunday after the service, Lisa had been obliged to join her parents in the assembly line of goodbyes from the parishioners, too. As always, she found she did not like that particular duty any more now than she had as a child. All those searching looks amid meaningless chitchat, and those long, pointy noses everyone felt free to stick into their pastor's family affairs. Yuck!

Her first Sunday home, Lisa had put on the outfit Dan Morgan had thought made her look like Eliza Doolittle. All set to take a stand, she had been more than surprised when neither of her parents had commented on it. The congregation had not disappointed her, however. Most of them had stared at her with expressions ranging from disapproval to downright hostility.

Let'em, she had thought with a mental thumbing of the nose. These days she was only a guest at the parsonage and didn't have to please those people anymore.

Isabelle Schulberg, the former mayor's snooty daughter whose castoffs Lisa, as a child, had been required to wear, had been her usual condescending self.

The name was Matthews now, she had lost no time informing Lisa. She had married Jake Matthews just this past summer. Did Lisa remember? Jake had been Pineville High's football hero. Later he'd gone on to WSU and almost made the varsity team there. Except he'd had to quit school to help with his father's *very* lucrative John Deere dealership.

And what was Lisa up to these days?

The question had been accompanied by another long, pointed look at Lisa's outfit. The look suggested that since Lisa was obviously still wearing hand-me-downs, she couldn't be too far removed from the gutter everyone had predicted she would end up in, living on her own in the big city.

Isabelle's comments had been the icing on a poisoned cake. Lisa couldn't help but dish out a piece of her own.

"Actually," she drawled with a bored little smile. "I just got my M.B.A. And I've accepted a choice job in the computer field. Misotec...you've heard of them, I'm sure—that group of young geniuses who revolutionized the software industry?"

At Isabelle's blank look, she allowed her smile to become superior and her brows to raise. She paused a beat as if waiting for a reply. When none was forthcoming, she said, "Surely, though, you *have* heard of the Morgan's Department Store chain?"

Isabelle's disdainful, "Of course. Who hasn't?" clinched it, as far as Lisa was concerned.

"Of course," she said. She leaned closer, detonating her bomb with a conspiratorial air. "I'm engaged to Dan Morgan. The heir."

The very instant those words left her careless tongue, Lisa regretted them. All the more so when, the minute they had her to themselves, her parents demanded to know why they had not been informed of this engagement before. It had taken extensive explanations on Lisa's part to convince them that there wasn't one. That Dan had been her employer, no more. Whereupon she had had to endure her father's ear-blistering lecture on the glory of truthfulness and the perils of deceit.

Remembering, Lisa smiled to herself as she followed her mother into the house. The entire episode might not have done much to demonstrate the maturity she had thought she'd attained in the past seven years, but it had been satisfying, just the same.

On entering the kitchen, the smell of roasting chicken was as familiar as the yellow cotton tablecloth and matching napkins her mother always used for Sunday dinner. Things never changed, it seemed, and yet they had.

Or was she the one who had done the changing?

The weeks with her parents had been peaceful, even relaxing. She had enjoyed their company and, if truth be told, had not minded Bible class all that much, either.

They had had long talks. Her parents had applauded her degrees and admitted their pride in her. They had talked of The Mission and of the good reports about her that the Reverend Thomas Murphy had sent every year.

They had talked about her job at Morgan's and about the circumstances under which she had broken her arm. She had told them that the man responsible for her injury was in jail awaiting trial, and her father had quoted on the wages of sin.

They had talked about all manner of things. Except Daniel Morgan.

She thought of him constantly, but in doing so had come to accept the fact that, though she couldn't change what she felt, neither were those feelings the end of the world. She had her degree—for two whole weeks now, at last! And the job at Misotec was waiting for her.

She had good friends—the twins. And John. And who knew...sometime in the future that average-looking, deep, socially aware man of her imagination just might show up. The prospect somehow was not as exciting as it should have been.

Dropping into a kitchen chair, Lisa yawned.

Her mother chuckled. "Still tired? And here I could've sworn you had a nice little nap during your father's sermon."

Lisa stared. "I . . . uh, how'd you know?"

"Same as I always knew." Jeanne scrubbed carrots, rinsed each one and laid it to drain on a pad of paper towels.

"The way your breathing evens out, and you sort of lean into me . . . like a sack of meal."

"Mom! D-does Pop—"

"Oh, no, don't worry. Here—" She handed Lisa a peeler, then took up another one for herself. "Help me peel these potatoes, will you, love."

They peeled in silence for a while.

"You never said anything," Lisa finally burst out. She'd been puzzling over the incongruity of it. Her sleeping in church; her father apparently never noticing; her mother seemingly condoning it. "How come I never got in trouble for it?"

"In trouble?" her mother exclaimed. "Why should you? It was such a little sin for such a good child."

"*Was* I a good child, Mom?"

"Of course you were." Jeanne smiled at her. "Most of the time, when your stiff-necked pride didn't trip you up."

"*When pride comes, then comes disgrace,*" Lisa quoted ruefully.

"Proverbs," her mother supplied.

They shared a laugh.

"Pop has a scripture quote for every occasion, doesn't he?"

"Occupational hazard. He means well."

"I know." They worked in silence for a moment.

"I really enjoyed your singing in church again today, Mom," Lisa said, at length.

"I'm glad." Her mother seemed content to follow Lisa's conversational lead. She leaned her head close and confided, "In my wild and wooly youth I used to perform in nightclubs, you know."

"I know. One of the boys told me once." Lisa frowned. "I always wondered how you could have given all that up to marry . . ." She faltered, not sure just how far to take this unaccustomed exchange of confidences. "I mean, singing in church hardly compares to singing in clubs...."

"Doesn't it?" Jeanne laughed, a gentle, happy sound. "If you promise not to tell your father—"

"Promise not to tell her father what?" Lucas Hanrahan thundered, causing the women to jump apart as he came into the kitchen on silent feet. "What deviltry are you up to, Mother?"

To Lisa's amazement, her mother just laughed. "Good gracious, Luke," she exclaimed, "you near scared me to death sneaking up like that. I was just going to mention to Lisa that singing in church is my favorite part of the service."

"Meaning you don't like my preaching?"

"Well..." Jeanne's tone and smile were almost coy. "There are times, Reverend Hanrahan..."

Lisa stood with her mouth open and her hands dangling in the sink while she watched her parents look at each other like... well, like lovers, of all things. And her mother was actually blushing.

She was quiet throughout their midday meal, content to observe her parents' interaction with each other. She was both happy and bemused by the discovery that they obviously loved each other and were content.

She had always assumed just the opposite to be true.

After they had eaten, her father lay down for his customary nap. Since Lisa would be returning to Seattle the following morning, her mother offered to help with the packing.

"I'm sure you'll be glad to get that cast off," she remarked as she folded the clothes Lisa handed her from out of the closet.

"And how." Lisa was once again trying unsuccessfully to push a finger up her cast. "I swear, bugs have begun to nest in there, I itch so bad."

"Means you're healing." Jeanne carefully placed each folded item into Lisa's suitcase. "What I'd really like to know, though, is how your heart is coming along?"

"I beg your pardon?" The hanger Lisa had just slipped off the rod clattered to the floor.

"When you first came home to us we could see you were in terrible pain," Jeanne went on. "In here." She indicated her heart. "I was hoping you'd feel like talking about it before you left?"

Lisa was too stunned to do more than stare.

"You knew?" she finally managed to choke out.

"Of course we did." Her mother rounded the bed and took Lisa in her arms. "You're our child—when you hurt, we do, too. Is it this...this Daniel Morgan you once mentioned?"

Lisa nodded, her cheek pressed against her mother's. "I'm so mixed up," she whispered.

"Will it help to talk about it, love?"

Lisa swallowed, shrugged. She kissed her mother's cheek and drew out of her embrace. With thoughts and emotions in a whirl, she walked over to the window. For long moments she stared down at the tidy snow-covered yard. The tall maple she had once gotten stuck in was stark in its winter nakedness and not nearly as intimidating as it had been years ago.

"I always thought you were unhappy," she finally said, almost to herself. "Married to Pop, I mean." When her mother made no reply, she half turned toward her and added, "You two seemed to be of such different worlds—you from show business and he...I don't know, such a stick-in-the-mud, for lack of a better term. I used to think you didn't match at all and I vowed never to make the mistake you made."

"And now?"

Her mother had come to stand next to her. Lisa inhaled her familiar lily-of-the-valley scent and savored this moment of closeness.

"And now," she said quietly, "I'm beginning to think I don't know nearly as much as I used to think I knew."

"That's maturity." Jeanne chuckled. She smoothed a fold of the dusty-rose drapes bracketing the window, glancing sideways at her daughter. "What else do you know now that you didn't before?"

"That you and Pop love each other."

"Ah. Smart girl." She abandoned the drape and, with a deep breath, crossed her arms in front of her again. "Though you were right in what you said earlier—we *are* two very different people. I like to think that's one of the reasons we never quite lost the spark."

She tossed her daughter another sidelong glance, this one full of warm smiles. "Am I shocking you?"

"Maybe a little." Lisa laughed softly, averting her eyes to her own fingers now pleating and unpleating a piece of the curtain. "A lot, actually. When I saw the two of you earlier today... you know, *flirting*—"

Her mother burst out laughing. A little sheepishly, Lisa joined in.

At length, Jeanne bit her lip and said, "A lot of what you felt was not so far off the mark, you know, back then. The Lord knows—" she shook her head and cast a heartfelt glance ceilingward "—the adjustments I had to make in those early years were not easy. As a minister's wife I felt like a failure as often as not. As a mother, some days it was all I could do to feed the lot of you.

"There was never enough money, enough time. The needs of the flock always had to take precedence. That was often hard for me to accept."

Jeanne glanced at Lisa as if in apology. "I was young. And it did get easier. And now... well, since you children left home, really, it's been very good. It's like it was with Luke and me in the beginning, before we were married. Better, in many ways, because now we're no longer quite so self-centered and self-conscious. We've both grown a bit more tolerant. Of our own, as well as each other's shortcomings.''

She reached out a hand and laid it against Lisa's cheek in a gentle caress. "Shortcomings—we all have those, my darling. One of yours was always a quickness to judge others by your own rigid standards.''

"It still is, I'm afraid." Lisa turned her face and nuzzled her mother's palm. She felt loving and loved. It felt good.

"Dan Morgan is...I love him." She covered her mother's caressing hand with her own, tried for a smile and failed. "But it's no good." She shrugged and pulled away. "We really are too different.''

"Are you? How?''

"Well..." Lisa went back to the closet, took another pair of jeans off a hanger. She felt very much out of her depth, and she wished desperately that what she was about to say was not true.

"For one thing, Dan's not in love with me." She avoided her mother's eyes, staring down instead at the bleached denim her fingers were crushing. "He, uh, doesn't approve of me. Not that I approve of him, generally speaking," she hastened to add with a quick glance at Jeanne who, Lisa noted with a hint of despair, was looking intrigued. Somehow she wasn't getting her point across.

"We don't have a thing in common," she reiterated more forcefully. "The man was born wearing silks and cashmeres while I—'' She tossed the jeans onto the bed. "More often than not, he considers me a charity case.''

"Oh?''

"It's like he thinks money is the answer to everything.''

"Well, it certainly can be, when judiciously spent.''

"Checks don't cook and clean and mend and heal, Mom. The hands of caring people do."

"True. But checks supply the tools your caring people work with, right? Don't discount the value of money, Lisa."

"I don't. I just don't glorify it. And I don't need *his*. He treats me like I'm some helpless ninny who isn't capable of walking and talking at the same time. When I'm perfectly capable of looking after myself."

Another pair of jeans was thrown after the first one. "You know, he fired me practically as soon as we met."

"Oh?"

"Well, it wasn't quite that cut-and-dried, but my point is, we're on opposite sides of practically every fence that matters."

"Sounds interesting."

"It isn't."

"Well, I'm sure you know best," her mother said mildly. She went to pick up and fold the discarded jeans. "Snobs and autocrats are best avoided, I suppose. Strange, though," she mused, "that you'd fall in love with someone like that."

Lisa frowned. "Dan's not a snob—"

"Merely condescending, hmm?"

"Well, no. He's—"

"A . . . what's the popular term? A chauvinist?"

"No. Actually, he's—"

"Generous? Assertive?"

Too late Lisa saw that she was caught in the morass of her own contradictory feelings. She hung her head and slowly nodded. "Yes."

Jeanne came to her. She coaxed Lisa's chin up with one gentle finger and looked into her eyes. "Would you say that you *liked* him before you ever knew you loved him?"

"Oh, Mom." Lisa closed her eyes, swallowed. "Yes."

"Well, then," Jeanne said, framing her daughter's face and gazing at it lovingly. "Given your inability to be objective about this man, how can you be sure the situation is hopeless?"

Lisa didn't answer, couldn't. But in her heart she knew it was.

Morgan's had been transformed into a glimmering, glittering mecca for the crowds of holiday shoppers. This season Lisa had been one of their number, searching out small gifts for friends and family, but mostly acquiring an appropriately businesslike wardrobe. The suits, shirts, sensible pumps and elegant dresses would have delighted Dan Morgan with their stylish simplicity.

Marcia, on the other hand, had laughed herself sick over what she termed Lisa's defection into yuppiedom.

Lisa tugged at the zipper of one of her new dresses. It was a bright red sheath the neckline of which was slashed in a deep V in front. The silky material hugged her trim form most flatteringly, and its rich color complemented her ivory complexion. She knew she looked good but couldn't get very excited about it.

She had been back from eastern Washington a week. The cast was off. On Monday she would start work at Misotec. She was even now getting ready for the celebration John, Marc and Marcia were putting on for her. She chided herself for being downhearted, told herself she had much to be happy about and thankful for. It was no good. She was miserable.

Still, once they arrived at the popular bar and eatery on the shore of Lake Union, Lisa tried to put on a good show for her friends. She laughed in all the right places, danced with John and Marc in the bar after dinner, even tried her hand at flirtation with some of the other men who asked her to dance.

And then she saw Dan.

He was dancing with a willowy blonde nearly as tall as himself. He appeared devastatingly handsome to Lisa's hungry eyes. As if physically feeling her avid inspection, he looked her way.

For the instant in which their gazes touched and held, all of Lisa's senses sprang to life. Her heart raced, her blood rushed hotly through her veins. Every muscle in her body was tensed and ready to propel her to his side.

And then Dan, his expression unreadable, nodded a polite greeting and looked away. The fleeting spell was broken, leaving Lisa shaken and bereft.

"Dance, Ms. Master's Degree?" Marc asked, his mouth close to her ear to make himself heard above the din of music, laughter and shouted conversations. John and Marcia were already weaving their way through the maze of tables toward the small dance floor.

Lisa forced a smile, shaking her head. "I'd just as soon sit this one out, Marc. My arm hurts a bit and it's such a crush out there. Someone might accidentally bump it."

"Sure, no problem. Mind if I ask the redhead over in the corner, then? She's been giving me the eye all night. Figure I might as well make her happy."

Lisa had to laugh in spite of her heavy heart. Modesty had never been Marc's strong suit. "No, I don't mind. You go ahead, spread it around. I'll just watch you operate. Maybe I'll learn something."

"Atta girl." Marc gently pinched her cheek as he got to his feet.

With amused indulgence Lisa watched him saunter over to the lucky redhead and bestow on her his gleaming pirate's smile—the one that brought out his set of dimples in full force. Taking the lady's hand in his, he helped her to her feet, all the while sinking smoldering looks into her adoring eyes.

"Looks like your friends abandoned you." Daniel's voice came from behind.

Lisa's head snapped around, her eyes up to his. Marc was forgotten.

"Mind if I join you for a moment?"

At her mute, negative shake of the head, he pulled out a chair and sat down.

"You're looking good," he said, knowing the words to be an understatement. She was stunning. A whole flood of words wanted to gush from his tongue—compliments, questions, entreaties... "I see your cast is off."

"Yes." For the life of her, Lisa could think of nothing suitably inconsequential to add to that. She would have liked to ask him if they couldn't still have that dinner he'd once mentioned. If he missed her at all, as she missed him.

"Thank you for paying the hospital bill," she said.

"Forget it." Dan impatiently waved her awkward and, on his part, unwelcome expression of gratitude aside. "I'm just glad you consented to let me do that much, at least."

His wayward gaze got momentarily tangled up in hers. Incredibly he thought he saw a fleeting expression of longing before she lowered her lashes. He drew in a deep breath, expelling it on the word, "Well," and racking his brain for something else to say. "So how've you been? All set to start your new job?"

"Yes." Lisa wrenched her thoughts away from the persistent what-ifs and might-have-beens they dwelt on. Her new job... Dan had used his influence there, too.

"It was good of you to make that call to Curt Dirkson," good manners prompted her to say, albeit not quite as graciously as someone else might have. At the time she had very much resented his interference and couldn't keep herself from pointedly adding, "Of course, I would have been perfectly capable of making my own arrangements."

"Of course." Dan's tone had an edge to it. "Nor could anyone be more aware or appreciative of your capabilities than I am. Even if you didn't take such pains to drive the point home at every turn. However, since you got hurt because of Morgan's, I wanted to make sure you didn't suffer undeserved hardships elsewhere."

"Yes, well…thank you," Lisa murmured, feeling gauche in the face of his genuine concern for her. "Mr. Dirkson has been very generous in holding the position for me."

"Well, good. Good."

Their eyes met again, lingered. Neither seemed able to look away. Nor did either of them seem able to identify the things they thought—and hoped—they saw.

"Are you happy, Lisa?" Dan finally asked softly.

"Happy?" The question caught Lisa off guard. She had just been thinking that Dan's eyes looked sad. "Everything I've ever worked for, dreamed of, is finally within reach," she hedged, adding brightly, "who wouldn't be happy, right?"

Was that disappointment she read in his eyes? She longed to lay her hand on his and say, "I should be happy, but I'm not. Do you love me?"

But of course, she said no such thing. What she did say, was, "What, uh, what about you?"

And was glad this once she'd curbed her too-quick tongue, when she followed the direction of Dan's quick glance and saw the blonde she had quite forgotten.

"As you said," he drawled. "When you've got it all together, who wouldn't be happy?"

"Right." Lisa forced a bright smile. And was immensely relieved to see John and Marcia coming back to the table.

Dan saw them, too. "I'd better be getting back to Gloria," he said, rising. "I just wanted to stop and see how you were."

"Thanks." Lisa's face was beginning to hurt from the effort of smiling. "Never better."

"Yes. Well—"

"Hi." Both John and Marcia offered the greeting rather breathlessly. "That was some dance," John puffed. "I'll bet I lost five pounds."

"Not that you needed to." Marcia poked a finger into his ribs and staged an outrageous leer.

"I like you, too, sugar," John hammed back.

Dan and Lisa avoided each other's eyes. A rather pregnant pause ensued before Dan cleared his throat and said, "Good to see all of you again."

"Same here," everyone chorused.

He looked at Lisa. "Take care of yourself."

"I will. Thanks."

"Great. I'll say good-night, then."

"Good night."

"Marcia. John." He nodded at the couple whose back and forth glances were troubled.

"G'night," they chorused, eyes focused now on Lisa's sorrow filled ones.

Dan knew Gloria had been closely watching him with Lisa. But he also knew that she considered herself much too sophisticated to ask questions. Which was one of the things he liked about Gloria.

He also liked the fact that she knew the score and would be ready—no, eager—to enter into any kind of relationship he might be willing to offer. He admired her taste in clothes. He appreciated that she knew when to speak and when to keep silent. Gloria was nothing at all like Lisa Hanrahan—which was what he liked about her best of all.

She would never prefer to do anything for herself. At least not when there was a convenient man around to do things for her. Not for her any causes, the feminist movement, the need to prove herself in a man's job. Nor was she one to refuse a gift or look down on wealth. On the contrary, she appreciated, even courted, both.

She was a woman with no ambitions to better the world, one who was content in her modeling career, one who limited her ambitions to maintaining a size-six figure and making the cover of *Vogue*. The ideal woman with whom to relax, one who would never drive a man out of his head with worry and guilt.

A woman who, unfortunately, on this their second date already threatened to bore him into a coma.

Approaching their table, Dan smoothed his brow and forced himself to return her smile.

"Trouble?" she asked, watching him take his seat across from her. "Most of the time you were scowling so fiercely at that poor little creature that she must have been scared to death."

"She wasn't."

Dan's lips twitched at Gloria's perception. Little did she know that particular "poor little creature" he had been verbally fencing with was able to flip him over her shoulder with the greatest of ease. And with just as little effort could reduce his insides to jelly.

"Well, I'm glad you're back."

Gloria reached across the table to capture one of his loosely clasped hands. Squelching the ridiculous feeling that he was acting like an unfaithful spouse, Dan let her cradle it between both of hers and forced himself to return her smile.

"I've missed you," she purred.

"I'm sorry I took so long," Dan apologized, gently tugging on his hand.

Gloria tightened her grip, lifting the hand she was holding and turning her face into its palm. Slowly, softly she pressed her lips into the sensitive hollow. The tip of her tongue flicked erotically, promising greater delights if only Dan would give the green light.

He didn't. Worse, he had no wish to, which made him angry. At Lisa. It was her fault for being here, for reminding him of everything he felt for her and had hoped to bury. What right did she have to make him feel guilty now? What right did she have to inhibit his perfectly healthy, normal, male responses in this way? None, by God.

"Let's dance," he said, pulling Gloria to her feet. As they snaked through the maze of tables toward the dance floor, he kept her defiantly clamped to his side. And when they started to dance, he did not retreat from the sinuous movement of her hips against his.

He hoped that—should Lisa be watching—the picture he and Gloria presented would show just how happy he was with the way things had worked out. His gaze swept the room, defiant, searching. And he was snagged by a pair of huge gypsy eyes that burned into his and seemed to brand him *traitor*.

Chapter Ten

I'll get it," Lisa yelled after the fifth ring had gone unanswered. She made a dash for the living room. En route she tripped over Marc, stretched out on the floor not five feet from the jangling telephone. He was engrossed in the football game on the thirteen-inch screen in front of him and oblivious to everything else.

Lisa shot him a glare as she scrambled across him for the phone and snatched up the receiver.

"Hello!"

"Ouch."

"Oh. It's you, John." Lisa's shoulders sagged with the puff of air she expelled. She dropped to the floor and sat cross-legged.

"Am I interrupting something? You seem about as glad to hear from me as you would from the IRS. Why don't I call back?"

"No, don't." Agitated fingers further mussing an already tousled head of hair, Lisa closed her eyes and worked at gathering her wits. You would think after all these weeks she wouldn't still be hoping every phone call was Daniel Morgan.

"I'm sorry," she said. "I'm just being my usual crabby self. On top of which I had to drop a tricky program I was working on to run for the phone."

"You alone?"

"I wish." She turned to look daggers at Marc, who still had not taken his eyes off the screen. She raised her voice. "Certain useless lumps on the floor don't know when they've worn out their welcome."

Marc half twisted toward her, brows raised. "You talking to me?"

Rolling her eyes in disgust, Lisa presented him with her back, saying to John, "Marc gave Marcia and me a TV for Christmas. Little did we know the giver's prone body would be part of the package."

"Bad case, huh?"

"Terminal." Across one shoulder she stuck her tongue out at Marc, who returned the favor as she added, "One hopes."

John chuckled. "And you such good company, too."

"Look, if you called just to be a wise guy . . ."

"I didn't," he said quickly, "so don't hang up." He gave a queer little laugh and cough. "I, uh, I'm calling on business, as a matter of fact."

"Business? What kind of business?"

"Security. Morgan's. And before you tell me you're no longer connected with either, hear me out."

At the mention of the name Morgan, Lisa had tensed again. Her foolish heart started to race and she wished she could order it not to. But wishing did her no good, just as wishing away her love for Daniel hadn't yet done any good.

"I'm listening," she said, taking pains to keep her tone neutral.

"Okay. Sooo." John drew out the word like a rubber expander before fairly snapping out the rest of what he had called to say. "How'd you like to take a little trip?"

"A trip? Where?"

"Anchorage."

"What?"

"Court. January second."

"What?"

"Is there something wrong with our connection, Leece? I can hear you fine, but you seem to be having a problem. Or am I suddenly speaking Swahili or something?"

"John." Lisa counted to ten. "I hear you, okay? It's just that you can't throw a trip to Anchorage at a person out of the blue and expect . . . I mean, what would *you* say?"

"*I'd* say whether or not I could go," John said. "It's not as if I'm asking without a good reason. You *are* the one who took care of that warehouse stuff with the boss back in September and now, uh, the case is finally on the docket. One of you has to go and testify."

"Okay," Lisa said agreeably, "so let Dan Morgan go. I've got obligations elsewhere. Misotec pays my salary, and guess what? They expect me to show up and work for it."

Darn it all, how could John put her into this position? Anchorage, of all places. All those memories . . .

"Why can't Dan Morgan go?" she repeated, a touch more belligerently as a cornered feeling made her squirm. "It's his store, his business. And he knows the case as well as I do."

"Morgan can't do it." John stopped to noisily clear his throat. "He would have gone, and he, uh, he really hated to ask it of you, Lisa, but he, uh . . . the flu. Yeah, that's it. He's got the flu."

Lisa frowned as she listened to another series of hacks.

"John, are you okay?"

"I'm fine. But Morgan isn't," John added quickly. "On top of being sick there's a real hassle with the California store. He'll probably end up having to go there...."

"I see." Lisa slumped. Her hand holding the phone was clammy with sweat. She did not want to do this. "You're sure you can't figure out something else?"

"Lisa. Be real. Would I bother you if I could? Anyway, they'll probably subpoena you. I'm just trying to save us all some time and trouble."

"Damn."

"I can't blame you for being upset." John's voice strengthened on a hopeful note. "But was that a yes?"

"I suppose."

"Great!"

John's immediate elation set Lisa's teeth on edge and when he added a cheery, "They say Anchorage is quite a pretty place. I'm sure you'll enjoy the trip," she exploded.

"Spare me the sales job, all right? I've been there, remember? It's a city, same as any other, period. Look." She expelled a long breath, fought to rein in her galloping temper. "If I'm going, I'd better clear it with my boss. I'll call you."

Slamming down the phone, she frowned fiercely at it. Just a city, she jeered. Oh, sure. Except that it was also the city in which she and Daniel had had such a wonderful time.... Though, of course, it was also the city where they'd had the whopping fight that had caused her to quit....

With a ragged sigh, she shook off the memories and picked up the phone.

Two hours and a series of calls later, all of the preliminary arrangements had been made and discussed. Misotec's offices were closed between Christmas and New Years anyway, and for something as important as court, Curt Dirkson had generously agreed to extend Lisa's vacation for however long the circumstances required.

John was downright gleeful. He assured Lisa that Morgan's would, of course, foot the bill for this trip, as well as reimburse any lost wages. He insisted she leave all the details to him.

He called the next day to say that everything had been taken care of. In spite of the holiday crush he'd been lucky enough to get her on a flight, as well as into a room at the Prospector's Inn.

Hearing the name, Lisa stiffened. "Can't you put me in another hotel? Last time I didn't really care for the service there."

She crossed her fingers at the fib. The fact was, she didn't relish this additional reminder of happier times.

John tut-tutted. "Sorry, Leece, no can do. The town's sold out. As it is, I had to throw some of Morgan's weight around to get you a room at all."

"Sold out? At this time of year? What's the attraction, for crying out loud?"

"Well, um . . ." John stopped to noisily harrumph before adding in a rush, "Dogsled racing."

Muttering unintelligibly, Lisa gave up. The entire expedition was sounding more and more ludicrous. Yet with Dan Morgan not only sick but also burdened with a score of other troubles, had there really ever been any question but that she would go?

"When do I leave?"

"You're not going to like this."

"John, my not liking things hasn't mattered so far, has it? When?"

"Tomorrow morning at ten."

"What?"

"Told you you wouldn't like it."

"Tomorrow is New Year's Eve."

"I know. And I feel terrible about doing this to you, Leece. Believe me. If it's any consolation, you'll be flying first-class, which oughta tell you just how important this is to Morgan's. I mean, you don't think for a minute they'd have sprung for that if there were any other way to get you there, do you?''

Lisa didn't. Still, her sigh came from right down in her toes. It wasn't that she had any special plans for New Year's Eve, but who wanted to spend it alone in a hotel room in Anchorage, Alaska? Or alone in a hotel room anywhere, for that matter?

She did not feel any better about it when, some twenty-four hours later, she was following the bellhop up to the fifth floor of the Prospector's Inn. The two of them had the elevator to themselves, which seemed odd in view of the hotel's allegedly sold-out state. The lobby had been all but deserted, too.

"I suppose most of your guests are out at the dogsled races." Lisa remarked to the freckled young man in charge of her one small suitcase and the key to the room.

He shot her a puzzled look, stepping out of the elevator and holding the door for her before responding. "I don't know about any dogsled races, ma'am, but if you're wondering why the place is so quiet, my guess is everybody who's able is someplace a lot warmer and sunnier than Anchorage, Alaska."

He chuckled, leading the way up the hall. "You here on business?"

"Yes, I am." Lisa's reply was automatic as she mulled over what he had said. No dogsled races? Her forehead puckered. But John had said—

"Are you telling me you're not sold out?" she asked.

"Sold out?" The bellman stopped at a door and inserted the key, laughing now. "Not hardly, ma'am. You and a few other unfortunate business types are about all we have in the house."

Preceding a thoroughly bewildered Lisa into the room, he
placed her bag on the luggage stand and opened the drapes.
"Course now, this evening things'll liven up a bit. A lot of
folks'll stay over after the big New Year's Eve party down-
stairs. If you're interested in attending, just call the desk."
On his way out the door, he stopped expectantly. "Will there
be anything else, ma'am?"

"No, thanks." She pressed a folded bill into his hand.

"Thanks, ma'am." Pocketing the tip with practiced
smoothness, the man inclined his head. "Have a pleasant
stay."

For long moments after hearing the door click shut, Lisa
stood in the center of the room. Gloom shrouded her like an
icy fog and made her shiver. Hugging herself, hands chaf-
ing the goose bumps on her arms, she moved slowly toward
the large window. Outside, snow-covered mountaintops rose
jaggedly into a cloudless blue sky, but she hardly noticed as
she stared blindly into the distance.

John had lied to her. About everything. The plane had
not been even half-full; she had seen plenty of available seats
in the coach section. And even before the bellman had said
anything, it had been clear as glass that the hotel was far
from booked up. Yet John had told her he had had to pull
strings to get her a room.

Why would he say stuff like that? Why would he lie to
her? None of it made any sense, unless...

Abruptly Lisa's eyes snapped into focus, and her whole
body tensed as she completed the thought.

...*unless someone very much wanted her here in
Anchorage now. Today.* Someone who thought she wouldn't
come unless there was absolutely no alternative. Someone
with sufficient authority to make John lie for him. Some
one like...

Dan Morgan.

Yes. Of course. It all made sense now. Hope surged. Not for a moment did she believe any longer that there really was a trial on January second. Dan had brought her here because...

She hardly dared to think the words, but they sneaked into her mind regardless. Dan had brought her here because he loved and missed her as much as she loved and missed him. There.

Laughing aloud, she whirled around once like a top, ran to the bed and flung herself backward down onto it, arms spread. What a crazy man he was, she exulted. What a dear, crazy man. She hugged herself fiercely, vowing that this time she would meet him halfway. She would sit on her stupid pride, if necessary, and apologize for the way she had acted that night in her hospital room. She would forgive him for the leggy blonde and not worry about their differences anymore.

"You were right, Mom," she whispered. "Everything will be just fine."

And it would. After all, he loved her; she loved him—they loved each other! Oh, Dan...

Dan. Lisa shot upright. Where was he?

Snatching up the phone, she punched O with a shaking finger and waited breathlessly for the front desk to answer. Dan had to be in this hotel, too, she reasoned, and as soon as she had his room number she would just pay him a little visit. No use leaving all the moves up to him, now that she was here.

Moments later, she slowly replaced the receiver. There was no Daniel Morgan registered, the clerk had assured her. Nor was there a reservation on the books.

Her spirits plummeted to earth and lower. So much for her fanciful imaginings of romance and intrigue, she thought bitterly. What an idiot she was, thinking that Dan Morgan would go to such lengths, spend all this money, just to stage some grand reconciliation with her. More likely he was even now getting ready to take that skinny model out to some New Year's Eve ball or other.

Furious, Lisa jumped off the bed and paced. Her lowered brows were separated by two vertical slashes as she walked, pivoted and stewed. Why couldn't she shake the feeling that things were not what they seemed?

The knock caught her at the window. Startled, she spun to stare wide-eyed at the door. *Dan.* Her heart soared up into her throat. She swallowed it down enough to make room for her voice.

"Who is it?"

"Bellman, ma'am."

"Oh." As swiftly as it had soared, her heart now dropped. She had to swallow again—bitter disappointment this time. "Just a minute."

She forced a smile as she opened the door to the same young man who had shown her up to the room earlier. He extended an envelope.

"The desk clerk forgot to give you this when you checked in."

"Thanks." Lisa accepted the letter without enthusiasm. Probably the subpoena John had mentioned. Closing the door, she leaned wearily back against it. She held the letter up so she could make out her name on the envelope. For one crazy moment she was tempted to pretend it contained an invitation to some fancy New Year's Eve party. But then, too weary to play games, she pushed away from the door and meandered back toward the bed.

She dropped down onto its edge, listlessly tore open the envelope and pulled out the single sheet it contained. It looked nothing like a subpoena. She read the few typewritten words twice before they made any sense.

"If you love Daniel Morgan, be at the Nugget Bar at 8 pm." No signature.

Good Grief! A ransom note.

The thought slammed through her brain like a jolt of live current and propelled her upward off the bed. Her heart pounded noisily in her chest, her knees quaked. She stared at the note in her shaking hand as if at a snake.

Who would send something like this? And why?

Bewildered, she read the words yet again. She lowered her arm, her brow slowly furrowing as she stared into space and tried to think rationally.

It couldn't be a ransom note. It just couldn't be. After all, who knew she would be here besides…wait a minute. Wait just a gosh darn minute!

Daniel Morgan. Of *course*! Who *else*?

Telling her foolish heart to stop acting like a demented yo-yo, Lisa decided things made perfect sense now. Dan Morgan was behind this entire charade.

That man!

Suddenly furious once more, she banished the jolt of joy and forced grimness onto lips still curved in a smile. Who did he think he was, she fumed, reaching and yanking her sweater up over her head. How dare he play games with her like this? How dare he?

She dragged off her jeans and dispensed with her underwear as she stomped into the bathroom to shower. Her hands shook as she turned on the spray. They were itching, she told herself, just itching to wring Dan Morgan's neck.

Dan's eyes' saw, but his mind didn't register the nearly deserted streets of downtown Anchorage. He drove his rental car as if on automatic pilot while his thoughts centered darkly on Lisa Hanrahan. Not that she hadn't been on his mind in some way or other ever since the day of their very first stormy encounter. But this was different.

Today he was angry. Really angry. Angry because in spite of everything that pointed to the contrary he had always

nurtured the secret conviction that Lisa cared for him. That
she only didn't know it yet. He was angry because he had
been girding himself for a showdown with her. One in which
he would bare his soul, declare his love and, if necessary
physically shake a similar confession out of her.

Well, not anymore. Miss Hanrahan's actions in refusing
John Turner's plea to handle the Anchorage court case
loudly proclaimed her indifference not only to Morgan's
but to Dan personally. She had known about the potentia
mess he'd have to deal with in L.A., but it had made no
difference. In fact, John had told him that he'd even gone
so far as to lie to Lisa, telling her that he, Dan, was sick with
the flu. And still she had refused to make this trip for him
According to John, "Too bad" had been the gist of her re
ply.

Just thinking of it, fury surged again. Dan jerked the car
into the driveway of the Prospector's Inn. His foot slammed
on the brake. The car rocked to a stop beneath the portico
He scrambled out.

They'd better have a room, he thought ominously, rel
ishing the thought of an argument in case they didn't
Morgan's was a good customer, by damn. There'd just bet
ter be a room. He shouldered through the double plate-glass
doors into the lobby, continuing his inner diatribe.

Reservations? Who'd had time to make one? He hadn'
even known till that morning he'd be coming to this god
forsaken place. Turner hadn't hung around long afte
dumping the news on him, and he'd spent hours trying to
find someone who could change the damn court date. Talk
about an exercise in futility—not a soul around who knew
what he was talking about. So what if it was New Year'
Eve? Whatever had happened to an honest day's work?

"I need a room." Dan's chin jutted out, his tone wa
laced with challenge. His hands on the reception counter
were balled into fists.

"No problem." The desk clerk's smile was pleasant. He indicated the registration form and added, "Any preferences? Perhaps a nice view?"

Dan muttered through clenched teeth and scrawled his name on the form.

Reading it, the clerk produced an envelope along with the room key. "This telefax come for you a short while ago, sir."

"Thanks." Dan gruffly pocketed both, shouldered his garment bag and waved the bellboy away. "I can manage this. Just park my car."

He hefted his briefcase and strode toward the elevator before the man could say anything further. Right then all he wanted was solitude—and maybe a bottle of Scotch from room service. It had been a bitch of a day.

The idea of a ripping good drunk steadily gained in appeal. By the time he hung his bag in the closet and dropped his briefcase onto the vanity-desk it had become a firm resolution. What better way to bid farewell to both the old year and his corny illusions?

He dragged off his overcoat and tossed it across the back of a chair. Reaching for the phone, he caught sight of the envelope sticking partially out of a pocket. He plucked it out, turned it over and wondered who would send him a fax when a phone call would have been cheaper and more efficient?

Shrugging, he ripped it open and pulled out the sheet of paper inside. A flick of the wrist snapped it open. Quickly he scanned the single sentence.

"If you love Lisa Hanrahan, be at the Nugget Bar at 8 pm." That was it. No signature. Nothing at all to indicate who had sent it or what it meant.

He lowered the note and stared into space, thinking. The tone of the message was curt with a hint of "or else." Could someone hostile—the warehouseman Lisa and he had nabbed, for instance—be planning some act of retribution for Lisa unless the charges were dropped or something?

Dan reread the message. Slowly. And shook his head. No. Wilson had no way of knowing he loved Lisa Hanrahan. Nobody knew that. Except possibly...

Face grim, Dan snatched up the phone and stabbed out John Turner's home phone number. In the course of their working relationship these past couple of months he had come to know it by heart. When even the tenth ring produced no answer, he swore softly, severed the connection and, after only a moment's hesitation, stabbed out another number.

"Hello." In his present mood, Marcia's sultry voice grated.

"Dan Morgan here," he said curtly. "Is Lisa—"

"Dan!" Marcia's delighted squeal was even more irritating. "Are you—oops." She giggled. Dan cringed. "I mean, *where* are you?" she cooed breathlessly.

Dan's brows beetled. Irritation receded and was replaced by something else. Suspicion. "Where do you think I am?" he countered slowly.

"Um—"

A rustling sound and muffled background voices had Dan's ears all but standing at attention. "Marcia?" he prompted.

"Um—yes?"

"Is Lisa there?"

"N-n-*yes*."

Dan willed himself to patience. She had been about to say no, he'd bet on it. Especially in light of the fast and furious background whispers.

"Could I speak with her, please."

"S-speak with her? Well, um... *what*?" More muffled whispers. "Oh. Dan? She's in the tub right now. Can I take a message?"

For Dan the urge to laugh had grown steadily through-out their exchange, as had the conviction that the twins, at least, were up to something. Given everything else, however, he was sure John Turner was involved, too.

Those son of a guns! Dan rocked back on his heels and chuckled quietly up to the ceiling. He would bet his store the three of them had cooked up some cockamamy plot to get him and Lisa together.

"Marcia?" he said, snapping back onto the balls of his feet, anxious now to end the call and make another. "Just tell Lisa Happy New Year for me, will you? And the same to the rest of you, too."

The moment the dial tone came on, he punched "Operator."

"Miss Hanrahan's room," he said, fingers crossed behind his back.

"Just one moment, please."

Grinning, Dan dropped the receiver back onto its cradle. He rubbed his hands, checked his watch. Seven o'clock. Whistling, he strolled into the bathroom for a quick shower.

Almost an hour later he critically eyed himself one last time in the mirror. He grimaced at the stuffy picture he made in his gray business suit, white shirt and maroon tie. Not quite what he would have worn for the occasion, given a choice, but then he had not been. He had come prepared to go to court, not to go courting.

Courting—good grief. What if she wouldn't have him? He forced the thought away and squared his shoulders. Sucking in one more fortifying breath, he left the room wreathed in outward calm while his insides quaked like underdone tapioca pudding.

He thanked the stars that let him be the only passenger in the elevator, for he didn't think he would be equal to even the barest of civilities. Two floors down, his fleeting luck ran out. He kept his eyes on the numbers overhead as the doors swished open, hoping his stance would convey his disinclination to be sociable.

His peripheral vision registered a couple in evening wear even as the woman's cloying perfume enveloped them all. Several more party goers came aboard on the sixth floor and when they stopped again on five, Dan was all but flattened against the elevator's back wall. He blessed his superior height: it allowed him to breathe air not quite so polluted by the clash of rivaling scents.

His breath got stuck in his throat, though, when Lisa was the one who entered the elevator on five. She smiled nervously at the group at large, and turned face front as the doors hissed shut.

Dan's mouth had gone dry at his first glimpse of her. Had she always been this beautiful? Though she was dressed much as he was in a no-nonsense business suit of deep maroon over a pink shirt, she had softened the outfit's austerity by artfully draping a large paisley silk scarf over one shoulder and across her breasts. All he could see of her as they descended toward the lobby was the shiny riot of her dark curls. His eyes stayed riveted on them. And all the while, his pulse raced and his heart thumped so loud he marveled that nobody turned to stare at him.

At lobby level, Lisa was the first one out. Everyone else followed at a snail's pace, talking and laughing, blocking the way for people like Dan who were in a hurry. By the time he had managed to squeeze and shoulder his way out, Lisa had almost reached the Nugget Bar's saloon-style swinging doors. She marched as if into battle, head high, shoulders straight.

Or maybe she was afraid that if she slowed she would lose her nerve and turn back.

A surge of tenderness closed Dan's throat as he saw by her gradually lagging steps that the latter was undoubtedly the case. He picked up his own pace as she stopped moving altogether just outside the entrance. The quick glance she tossed back in his direction was wide-eyed and uncertain. It moved past him without recognition, then snapped back.

Dan stopped in the middle of the lobby, his eyes locked on hers. He watched them grow large as black saucers, kindle with all manner of glad, delightful fires—and abruptly narrow.

"Dan Morgan!" He saw rather than heard her exclaim his name, transfixed as he was by the lightning change in her. Eyes flaming with anything but gladness now, she snappily reversed her previous course and marched toward him.

"So it *was* you who set this up," she hissed from just beneath his nose. "I *knew* it!"

She was past him, running, and almost in the elevator by the time Dan had roused himself sufficiently to give chase. The doors were closing when he got there. He forced them apart and slipped inside.

"Now, then," he growled, incensed. He hauled her hand off the "close door" button and spun her around to face him. "Would you care to tell me what that was all about?"

"No." She yanked out of his grip and flounced away. She folded her arms across her chest, her expression mulish.

"All right." Dan punched eleven, his floor. "Then how about explaining to me what you're doing in Anchorage? Or are you too cowardly to do that, too?"

"Cowardly?" Lisa dropped her arms and spun to face him again. "I'm not the coward here, you are!"

"Meaning?" Dan lounged back against a side wall, brows at an arrogant tilt.

"How could you?" Lisa exploded. "How could you drag me all the way to Anchorage on some pretext rather than simply call me up at home and say you love me. Do you realize the trouble—"

"Whoa!" Dan snapped away from the wall. "Back up a minute. What do you mean, 'love you'?" He stuck his nose into her face. "Who says I love you?"

The elevator stopped on eleven. The door glided open. Dan and Lisa neither noticed nor moved. Their eyes dueled; their lips were compressed in almost identical lines of stubbornness.

"The note says—"

"Don't give me 'the note says.' I'm here to go to court, nothing else."

"Oh." She looked nonplussed—hurt?—for just the merest heartbeat before flinging out, "Well, so am I."

The elevator door closed, unnoticed. They descended.

Dan said, "I see. And you always hang out in hotel bars at night, is that it?"

"I was in the lobby, not the bar."

"Semantics."

"Fact."

"What were you doing there?"

"Where?"

"Lisa, so help me—"

All at once Dan's beleaguered patience ran out. With a muttered oath he gripped her upper arms and hauled her body against his. He dipped his head and covered the startled O of her mouth with his.

Lisa's resistance was fleeting and merely born of surprise. She stiffened just slightly, then succumbed to the heady, longed-for pleasure of Dan's lips on hers. She reached for his strong shoulders and clung, feeling like a drowning person going under for the third time. She was befuddled, in tune with past, present and future all at once. Dizzy with love. And with wanting.

The elevator stopped. The doors opened. They kissed on, oblivious.

Wanting. Dan was consumed by it as he devoured the sweetness of Lisa's lips. This was it. This was his dream. To have her in his arms again. To make her his. Irrevocably.

She loved him. He felt it in her every move. In the way she raised her tiny frame on tiptoe all the better to fit it to his. In the way she shaped her mouth, opened it, all the better to give his tongue access to hers. In the way their tongues met, entwined, mated. The way their lips feathered, nipped, fused.

As effectively as a bucket of water extinguishes fire, a sudden burst of cheers and applause ripped the sensuous haze in which they were wrapped. Dan and Lisa broke apart. They blinked in owlish bewilderment at the crowd in the lobby in front of them.

The lobby? How had they gotten there?

Their gazes snapped back to each other's flushed faces. Mirth burst from them as if on cue. Laughing, they faced their audience and, again as if on cue, they bowed deeply from the waist.

Amid shrill whistles, laughter and applause, Dan punched "eleven" once more and, when the doors were closed, turned back to Lisa.

He was deeply touched by the mixture of vulnerability and challenge he read in her eyes. Now that they were alone in the aftermath of their telling kiss it almost seemed as if she were waiting for him to deny his love for her again. Yet, at the same time, she seemed to be daring him to do so.

"I do love you," he said, his voice husky with the wealth of feelings she aroused in him. Love, fierce and protective, though she wouldn't thank him for the latter. Love, steadfast through fun as well as strife. Love, hotly wanting, carnal.

His mouth felt parched with his thirst for her as he watched a dazzling brilliance replace all other expression in her eyes.

He cupped her shoulders, held her there in front of him. "Tell me," he said in a throaty whisper, feeling vulnerable himself suddenly. He needed to hear the words from her, too. "Tell me why you were going to the Nugget Bar?"

"Because—" Lisa stopped, swallowed, reached up to tremblingly touch his cheek. Suddenly, giving voice to what was in her heart seemed like the most difficult thing she had ever done. Not because she wouldn't mean the words, but because she would. They would be a commitment, and one she would need from Dan in return. She looked into his eyes, searching. What she saw gave her courage.

"Because I love you, too, Dan," she said.

"Oh, my darling." Dan pulled her all the way to him then, wrapped his arms around her and just stood like that, slowly rocking with her. They savored each other's nearness for a moment, and then Dan sought her lips in the sweetest of kisses.

"We need to talk," he said when they could stand to draw apart a little.

"I know."

They kissed again, instead.

"I want to marry you, Lisa." Dan searched her eyes. "Will you . . . ?"

Lisa knew no doubts just then, only hope. And love. "Yes." She curled her fingers around the nape of his neck and met the electric blue fire in his eyes with equal fervor reflected in hers. "Oh, yes."

"When?"

"Now. Tomorrow. Anytime you say."

The elevator stopped on the eleventh floor. The doors slid open. Without lifting his lips from hers, Dan shuffled Lisa backward out into the hall. Still kissing her, he scooped her up into his arms, walked with her to his door, unlocked it and carried her through.

Inside, savoring every moment, Dan let Lisa's body slide slowly down the length of his until they stood hip to belly, toe to toe. He looked down into the darkly shimmering pools of her eyes and felt he could drown in their soft, sparkling depths.

With her hips intimately pressed against him, he felt he could burn to cinders from the passionate heat his body radiated.

"You know we'll probably fight a lot, don't you," he said, remembering fires between them that had not been kindled by passion.

"I know. Do you mind?"

"Not if we can spend hours afterward making up."

"Like this?" Lisa raised on tiptoe and kissed Dan's mouth with lingering, newly acquired sensuality and expertise.

"Not quite," Dan breathed against her lips.

"Then show me," Lisa said, feathering kisses along his jaw and chin.

"I will. I promise. But first we have some talking to do—just so there's no confusion later."

He steered her toward the bed, sat with her on its edge, his arm across her shoulders keeping her clamped to his side.

"Should I be alarmed?" Lisa murmured, leaning over to press a kiss onto his mouth. "My father always warned me—"

"Forget your father and his commandments, all right? I won't do anything he wouldn't approve of."

"Too bad," Lisa said, pressing closer.

"Brat." Their lips, hot and eager, fused. Their hands stroked, searched. Their hearts raced; their bodies strained. And then, with a groan, Dan pushed Lisa away and stood up.

"Talk," he said, his voice husky and not quite steady. Nor was his hand when he pulled a school ring of heavy gold from his pinky and slipped it onto Lisa's middle finger.

"This will have to do for a day or two," he told her, "until I can get you something more permanent. Since I only intend to get married once in my life, I want everything to be done just right. Everything."

He waited until Lisa raised her glowing eyes to his before adding, "Do you understand what I'm saying?"

She nodded, the smile she gave him tremulous. "Yes."

"We'll have a proper wedding, in church—"

"With my father officiating?"

"Who else?" Dan kissed her nose and sat down next to her again. Their hands remained tightly clasped.

"Nothing fancy," Lisa warned, adding, "And I want some of my friends from The Mission to be there."

"Only if I can invite some of mine from the country club."

"F-fine." There was a pause. Lisa fidgeted.

"Dan, I won't stop my work at The Mission," she finally said. "So don't ask me."

"I hadn't planned to."

"Oh. Then will you come with me?" Lisa craned her head around to look into his face. "And help?"

Dan hesitated only briefly. "If you'll come along with me to my clubs. Learn to play golf, and bridge, and tennis...."

"Daniel, no! I couldn't." Lisa wanted up and out of his arms, but he wouldn't let her go. "That's not my scene at all."

Dan said nothing. Only waited.

Lisa stared beseechingly up at the ceiling. No help came from there, either. "Do I have to?" she finally sighed.

"What do you think?"

She thought of her mother. Compromises. She sighed again, heavily. "I think I should probably give it a try."

Dan squeezed her hands. "You might even learn to like it. *And* make all kinds of new friends."

"I like the friends I already have...."

"So do I... which reminds me. How do you propose we punish them for hatching this devious plot?"

They spent a few enjoyable minutes scheming various forms of torture and revenge for John Turner and the twins. But in the end they decided what they really owed those three was thanks.

"Still, they shouldn't get off scot-free. After all, they did cause us some very stressful moments. How about we make them baby-sit our spoiled-rotten kids?" Dan suggested with a chuckle of anticipation. He kissed the top of Lisa's head nestled in the crook of his shoulder. "How does that sound?"

"Kids?" This time when Lisa struggled to get free, Dan let her go. He watched her move away a few paces, then turn to face him, frowning. "How many, and how soon?"

"A couple. Anytime." He made to reach for her hand, but she snatched it away.

"Dan, this is serious." She paced again, stopped, faced him with a mixture of defiance and challenge. "I've just gotten started in my career. I don't intend to give it up."

"Ever?" Dan, too, was on his feet. His expression was one of incredulity and shock.

"Well, no. Dan, how can I, when I've worked so long and so hard to get where I am. How can I stop?"

"You don't want children?" he asked slowly.

"Not right away, no."

"And later?"

"Later we can discuss it again."

"We'll discuss it now, Lisa."

Suddenly they were nose to nose, glaring at each other. Voices rising.

"I won't give up my job, Dan."

"Did I ask you to?"

"You said—"

"I said I wanted children."

"So—"

"So it's possible to have both, Lisa!"

"You're shouting at me!"

"I'm not shouting, you are!"

They jerked apart. Exchanged glowers. Crossed their arms and turned their backs on each other. Fuming.

Silence.

"Are we fighting?" Lisa finally asked the wall to her right.

"Yes." It was Dan who replied.

"I don't like it, do you?" Lisa said.

"No."

"I've been thinking."

"Oh?"

"Yes. About compromises. And I've been thinking that I could probably work part-time, right? While the kids are little?"

"Sounds reasonable." They had turned as they spoke and were facing each other again. Their eyes met and clung. Slow, rueful smiles replaced the frowns.

"So, uh—" Lisa chewed at her lip, looked away, down at her hands. She fiddled with the heavy ring that was much too loose even on her middle finger, twisting it around and around. "Do you think you could, you know... show me how to make up now?"

She lifted her eyes with an impish grin. "Please?"

Dan's shout of laughter was full of delight. "Come here, you," he growled, extending his hand.

And Lisa took it. For life.

*   *   *   *   *

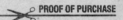

SILHOUETTE·INTIMATE·MOMENTS®

**Premiering in September,
a captivating new cover
for Silhouette's most adventurous
series!**

Every month, Silhouette Intimate Moments sweeps
you away with four dramatic love stories rich in
passion. Silhouette Intimate Moments presents
love at its most romantic, where life is exciting
and dreams do come true.

**Look for the new cover next month,
wherever you buy Silhouette® books.**

2IMNC-1

 *Silhouette Books®*

Double your reading pleasure this fall with two Award of Excellence titles written by two of your favorite authors.

Available in September

DUNCAN'S BRIDE
by Linda Howard
Silhouette Intimate Moments #349

Mail-order bride Madelyn Patterson was nothing like what Reese Duncan expected—and everything he needed.

Available in October

THE COWBOY'S LADY
by Debbie Macomber
Silhouette Special Edition #626

The Montana cowboy wanted a little lady at his beck and call—the "lady" in question saw things differently....

These titles have been selected to receive a special laurel—the Award of Excellence. Look for the distinctive emblem on the cover. It lets you know there's something truly wonderful inside!   DUN-1

Take 4 bestselling love stories FREE

Plus get a FREE surprise gift!

COMING SOON...

For years Harlequin and Silhouette novels have been taking readers places—but only in their imaginations.

This fall look for PASSPORT TO ROMANCE, a promotion that could take you around the corner or around the world!

Watch for it in September!

★